Immortal Island Series

1st installment Spellbound
Available now online

2nd installment The Vampire Masquerade
Available now online

By

S.L Ross

The Fallen

†

Now that it's over,
My worlds forever changed.
Without you, I feel empty,
All this pain remains.

S.L Ross

𝔍mmortal 𝔍sland – 𝔗he 𝔉allen · 𝔙olume 3

This is a work of fiction. Names, characters, places and incidents either are the product of the author's imagination or are used fictitiously. Any resemblance to actual persons, living or dead, events, or locales is entirely coincidental.

PRINTED IN USA

ISBN-13: 978-1466389861
ISBN-10: 1466389869

Prologue

Hierarchy

Following Alaina's birth...

As Erick entered through the large golden doors of the Hierarchy, his heart raced with every step. The Watchers, his superiors, were demanding to speak with him at once. Avoiding their calls lasted only so long before they summoned him without choice. The great hall, a place he used to call his home; large white and gold trimmed doors open upon his arrival. Instantly he felt the burning of their unwelcoming stare. As he stood in the doorway, he looked up to find all eyes of the Archangels were on him, yet no one spoke. Erick made his way to the altar. With respect, he bowed.

"Your Eminence," He bowed his head to him.

His back was to Erick, "Did you not pledge allegiance to the Almighty?" He asked, his voice echoing in the vast room.

Erick felt shamed and hung his head as he answered, "Yes."

"Did you not vow to protect the prophecy at all cost, even if that meant ending your own life?" He asked.

"Yes." His face burned with embarrassment.

"Then why has it come to this Eremiel?" He questioned.

"What do you mean?"

"You have fallen for the human girl—again." He scorned.

"I have not."

He scowls, "You were never to interfere, unless she was in danger. You were never to speak with her, not even to accept gratitude for your rescue efforts." His deep rumbling voice shook the room. Erick could not answer. "When I reassigned you Eremiel, that meant you no longer had any attachment to her. Yet, you deliberately disobey the order and continue to go to her. She accepted her fate, therefore the prophecy is destroyed!" He turned to face him, "You have forsaken us Eremiel. Your actions are deplorable!"

"She did not choose her fate it was bestowed upon her, without her consent. I could not bear to see her go in a wrong way, with that beast who took her." His eyes welled but he did his best to choke back the tears. Weakness was not something they want to see. "She has remained kind and generous—"

"She has taken a life Eremiel! Do not be swayed by their ability of persuasion. She is unworthy of our protection now!" His chest heaved, he turned away, "Let the beast have her."

"No!" Erick screamed. All heads turned to look at him and scowl, "Please Azazel—"

He interjects, "You shall not see her again, for if you do, you shall suffer the consequences." He said angrily. "Have I made myself clear?"

"But—"

"IS THAT CLEAR!" His voice filled the room with thundering crackles. "Do you wish to live among the humans as an outcast, as one of the fallen, to die among them and not your brethren?"

"No—please, I will do anything you ask. I will repent." Erick begged.

"Repent? There is no amount of repenting that will deem you worthy of the Archangel entitlement!"

Erick begged, "Your Eminence, please, let me prove to you—"

Azazel interjected, "No! Leave my sight before I change my mind and banish you forever." Erick could not move. Then as he turned to leave, like a dog with his tail tucked between his legs, Azazel added, "Unless . . ." Erick's heart raced and he wanted to take back his last few words. That tone of Azazel's voice made him very wary of what was to come next. His eyes widened in anticipation. "You kill the child." He replied craning his neck to look at Erick.

"What?" He gasped suddenly feeling faint. Erick did all he could to stand still, "I can't do that! You ask of me an impossible task."

"Is it Eremial? Or is it that you are blinded by your love for the girl? If you want to prove to me, that the love of your God is stronger than the love of her child—then kill the abomination before it is too late." He demanded. Azazel's eyes narrowed and he examined Erick closely. "That is your task, take it or leave it. There are no more second chances Eremiel!" Once again, he turned his back to Erick. Azazel began speaking with the other angels in a hushed voice. Erick knelt once again, crossed himself, turned and left with the doors sealing shut behind him.

His mind was all over the place. How could he kill Alaina, after everything Sarah has been through? She would never forgive him. From the moment, he had first laid his eyes on her, his world changed. She was the most beautiful creature to have walked this earth. The first time that he felt his heart ache for her, he knew he would be in trouble.

The elders kept a close eye on her and now it meant they were watching closely. Unless she called for Erick, he would have to remain at a distance. There was no room for mistakes. There had been too many close encounters already. If not for fear of losing his wings, he would have vowed his undying love to her long ago.

It had been several weeks since he had heard from Sarah. Not once, had she called for him since she left the island. The last time he had seen Sarah, it did not end well. They had an intimate encounter, in a moment of weakness, on his part. He opened his heart to her when he should have walked away. Now, her touch haunts him every day that they are apart. He longs for her so much that he would risk everything, to be near her. However, he was her guardian, not her lover and it had to stop, before it went too far. Since that moment, he had distanced himself from Sarah. If he lost his wings now, there would be no one to protect her. Vampire or not, he loved her. Now, she spent her days with Ambrose, which made it hard to find her. He held her somewhere with heavy magic protecting their location. To occupy his mind, he spent most days helping his other Charges.

When Erick did eventually find her, she was fleeing from the Werewolves that had taken her daughter.

Erick once again felt helpless. There was nothing he could do to stop them. That pushed her even farther away from him. The look Sarah gave him before she left that day, tore him up inside.

Weeks later, Ambrose showed up at his front door with Sarah. Angry and irrational, leaving Erick with little choice but to lock her up in his cellar until she calmed down. She risked everyone's life including her own, by going against their advice. Now, Alaina is out of reach and they must ask for more help than ever before. Erick could not bear the thought of locking her up, but it was his only choice. Her screams still haunt his nights.

Chapter One

Sarah

'Sssaaraaahhh.' A voice whispered . . . .

    Golden rays of sunshine, shone through the window and onto the bed, where I slept. Tiny flecks of dust, danced in the air around me. The room was medieval; everything was made of wood and velvet, in rich colours of red, gold and navy blue. It was a nice change from the cold damp cellar I had come accustomed to these recent weeks. I pulled off the heavy down filled duvet and got out of the bed. The hardwood floors were warm under my feet. There were slippers by the door so I slipped them on and walked out to the hallway. I walked through the maze of hallways until I reached a set of stairs and descended. The scent in the air was familiar. I let it guide me. There were voices in the kitchen and when I entered, Erick was making breakfast. His back was to me. I walked closer and someone stepped out of the shadows.

"Chase?" I gasped. He just smiled at me but there was a terrible pain in his eyes. I touched Erick on the shoulder and when he turned to face me, all I saw was a giant rat face.

"SQUEAK!" He said and I screamed jumping back.

'Saaaraahhh help me.' The voice pleaded.

I woke up gasping and screaming, a rat scurried around searching for food, making a hell of a lot of noise for such a tiny creature. I choked back a laugh and kicked the rodent away from me. The streak of sunlight burned my eyes forcing me to crawl away. The pain in my head was unbearable. I thirsted badly. The whispering voice must have been brought on by lack of blood. I lost track of how long I had been down here. I needed to drink something before I lost my mind all together. There was a shuffle on the other side of the door, a crumpling sound and then a bag appeared over my head through the iron bars of the cellar door. I turned on my side and looked up at it.

"I have taken the liberty of getting a few things for you before we head out." Erick said.

"What makes you think that I want anything from you?" I steadied myself, on my feet. I leaned against the wall, out of his line of site.

"Get dressed." He chuckled.

Just the thought of his lips curved ever so perfectly smiling at my demise, infuriated me. Something terrible was happening inside me. This anger taking hold was so overpowering. Just the thought of him being outside that door made me want to break it down and kill him. I don't know if that were the effects of Ambrose's blood kicking in or my humanity disappearing.

"No." I snarled and turned away from the door.

"Sarah, just get dressed." He replied dropping the bag.

"First of all, I'm filthy. Secondly, I'm starving, are you sure want to let me out? And lastly," I grabbed the bag tearing the plastic and staring him in the eye through the iron bars, "I am not going anywhere with you!" I growled and tossed the clothes back at him through the bars. I gripped the metal and shook the door. "Let me out of here now!" The door unlocked. I turned the handle and pushed the door open. Erick stood there waiting, his eyes locked on mine. Slowly, I made my way out.

I was tempted to run but my body was still too weak and I practically collapsed. Erick helped me to my feet, his touch angering me. "How could you?" I cried. If I could, I would have ripped his throat out right there. The thought of ripping his neck open and drinking his blood really appealed to me.

"You wouldn't." He said.

I stopped walking with him and pushed away.

"Don't do that." I stumbled but he grabbed me again. His hands cupped softly against my cheek.

"Sarah—I'm truly sorry that you are angry with me, but it was for your own good." He teleported me to the room from my previous stay here. "Have a bath, relax before we leave." He said opening the closet door. "We do not want anything bad to happen. You need to be of sane mind and body before we go anywhere." He walked back over to me and took my hand in his. "We have some leads but there are a few things we need to figure out first."

I slipped my hand out of his. "What leads?" I asked crossing my arms. He kissed my forehead and caressed my cheek. "Don't." I closed my eyes and gently pushed him away.

His eyes blinked rapidly, "We can discuss that later." He turned and walked towards the door.

"I thought you were no longer my guardian." My eyes narrowed.

"As of last week, when Ambrose dropped you here, I was no longer anyone's guardian." He explained his body turned halfway towards me.

"Oh—I'm—sorry." I said and glanced away. I ruined lives even while locked up.

"It was my fault really." He turned to face me, his brow furrowed. "I should have kept my distance from the start. Normally, I don't fall in love with my Charges . . . with you it proved harder than imaginable . . . There was no denying how I felt anymore." He stood by the bathroom door his hand on the handle. "I am just sorry that I couldn't stop what happened to you. Now, I don't know how vulnerable I am."

"So they left you defenceless?" I sat down on the bed to retain the strength I had left. My hand fell in my lap tears poured from my eyes effortlessly.

"No, I have some abilities just not the good ones." He chuckled and turned away from me. "I can't heal you, if you are injured and—I can die."

"Doesn't seem fair," I replied.

"I'll be fine. There are far worse feats, I would rather not face." He tried to smile but I notice the tremble in his lip.

"What—could be worse than losing your wings?" He stood there for a long time staring at me. The silence

that filled the room sent a chill through me. Afraid of his
answer so I averted my eyes.

"I'm surprised you have to even ask," He whispered.
His lips thinned and his eyes watered. My eyes grew
heavy and my heart began to palpitate. I clawed at my
chest. He cleared his throat and finally looked away. He
was not going to pull me back in, I won't let him. "I-I'm
s-sorry that, that happened to you." I stuttered.

"Don't be. There are ways to make it up to them. It
has been my first time on the outside of the glass house, so
to speak." He was trying to make me feel better, but every
time I looked into those fathomless green eyes of his, I felt
a pang in my heart. I hated this. All these mixed emotions
made me want to explode. He risked everything for me
and all I could think about was how much, I hated him
right now. My eyes filled with tears again and I glanced
up at the ceiling, wishing them away. Erick walked into
the bathroom. He turned on the tap and the rush of water
filled the silent room. Moments later, steam billowed out.
The water stopped and he exited the bathroom. I slowly
stood hugging the bedpost to steady myself before walking
over to the door. Erick lit a few candles for me before he
left. "I'll leave you to it." He said walking away.

I sat on the edge of the tub testing the water with my
fingertips. The amber light in the room gave off a very
warm and calming glow. Reminding me of a time when I
was human and the warmth of the bath soothed me after a
lousy day. I closed my eyes and tried to relax but the
pressure in my chest was becoming unbearable. The sobs
were trying to break free. Slowly, I peeled off my filthy
clothes but my mind was elsewhere. As the last piece of
clothing dropped to the floor, I felt warm fingers grasp my

arms and a gentle kiss touch my shoulder. I froze and gasped as his arms came around me slowly. It had been so long since I felt the warmth of his skin. I wanted him so bad but this was not the time. I reached from behind and caressed his face. His lips touched my palm. A tear trickled from my eye. I wiped the tears shutting my eyes tight as I gathered the words to say. I turned to face him, planted my palms firmly against his cheeks and kissed him softly then stepped away.

"I can't—I'm sorry." I said. His cheeks flushed with embarrassment. "I just can't think about anything else right now." I replied and stepped back.

He nodded averting his eyes, "I have something for you to drink when you are done." He whispered then left.

I climbed in the tub and submerged my entire body. My head floated slightly above the water. The sound of my breathing soothed me to sleep.

I don't know how much time had passed when I woke up fully immersed in the bath water. I sat up sloshing the freezing water everywhere. Once I regained my composure I pulled the plug then climbed out grabbing the towel off the rack. After brushing my hair I walked into the bedroom. Erick had laid some clothes out for me on the bed. I squeezed my eyes shut feeling unbelievably terrible for rejecting him earlier. Things were just too complicated right now. I have been through enough pain already. Besides, I have an uneasy feeling that will not go away. The voices in my head were not normal, even for me. Seeing things is one-thing but hearing voices that were not there, that's a whole other ball game. Then again, I still don't know if I was hallucinating or not. I wish the voice I heard was clearer so that I could figure out who was calling out to me. I have not mentioned it to

Erick yet, only because I had only heard it a few times and it was during the time that I was starving in the cellar.

Just as I thought that the voice whispered again.

'Sssaaaraaahh.'

I spun around facing the open window. No one was there and I sensed nothing. Maybe a ghost was following me. My entire body shivered. I dressed quickly then joined Erick in the kitchen. He handed me a glass filled with thick red liquid. The coppery sweet scent filled my nostrils immediately. "Sorry about earlier." I said reaching out to touch his hand but he pulled away. My lip twitched slightly.

"Don't be." He waved it off, "After what you have been through. I was stupid to think you would—"

"That is not what I meant." I gulped the entire glass down quickly. Closed my eyes as the blood raced through my veins. I stood up and walked towards him.

"Is there a ghost in this house?" I asked changing the subject.

"Not that I am aware of. Why do you ask?"

"Hmm," I said rinsing the glass.

"Sarah?" He pressed.

"It's probably nothing." I replied and sat down on the barstool. Erick pulled another bag of blood from the freezer and tossed it in the pot of boiling water.

"Well it must be something, if it is bothering you. Did you see something?" He asked.

"No." I answered shortly.

"Then why did you ask?" I watched him closely as he pulled the warmed bag of blood from the pot and cut the corner. My mouth salivated instantly.

"I heard—something." I screwed my lips at how ridiculously childish that sounded. "I heard it when I was in the cellar and I heard it after my bath."

"What did you hear?" he asked.

I watched as he squeezed the entire contents of the bag into the same wine glass.

"Someone calling out to me," I licked my lips.

"I haven't heard anything and I have lived here for decades." He replied handing me the full glass.

"It must be nothing." I shrugged it off and downed the second glass.

"Don't dismiss it just yet. Do you recognize the voice?" He asked.

"No, it just whispers my name," I licked my lips and dabbed the corner of my mouth.

"Thirsty?" he chuckled. I rolled my eyes. "If you hear it again, tell me. It could also be that you are hallucinating from lack of—blood."

"I thought that too." I sighed, sat back and watched him cook food for the first time. "I guess I will have to wait and see if I hear it again now that I have fed." I stood.

"Fed is not what I would call it. You have had two pints of blood, which is not nearly enough to sate a vampire's appetite. You may still feel sluggish or irritable." He said then turned around to grab his plate and I was standing right there. I slinked my arm under his and hugged him close. He did not hug me back but I refused to let go. He took a deep breath and held it. I slowly pulled away to look at him. Instinctively, I caressed his face.

"I do love you Erick." I whispered staring into his eyes my fingers ran through his hair. Yes, I was angry, but I love Erick. I know the feeling of anger towards him will pass. He had never hurt me before. Not like this.

His lips pressed thinly. I kissed him before he could pull away. "Have you heard from Ambrose?" I asked changing the subject.

"Yes—" he cleared his throat, "he is on his way." He replied sitting at the table.

"What did he have to say?"

"Not sure, he wouldn't say over the phone." Erick sat down with a plate full of food. He practically shovelled a mouthful in and then another.

"I—don't think I have ever seen you eat before." I chuckled then sat across from him.

"I'm human now, I have an appetite now." He smiled then looked down at his plate. He stared at the food a moment, as though he had something to say then filled his fork. This new awkwardness between us was going to destroy whatever feelings we had left for each other.

I leaned forward and touched his arm, "I don't think you should come with us." I said.

His mouth was full so he chewed a moment then said, "Are you crazy?"

"No. You are too vulnerable right now and I don't want to lose you." Before he could say anything, another voice replied.

"She is right. You would be a liability if anything." Ambrose leaned against the doorframe crossing his arms.

"That is not what I meant." I rolled my eyes as I craned my neck to look at him. He smiled at me like always. "Where is she?"

He shrugged, "I have no idea. Last I'd heard she was with the pack leader." He replied callously.

"Pack leader?" I replied. I leaned against the table with one hand and the other on my hip.

"The wolves still have her. They are refusing to give her back." He walked forward. "Maybe her father can help. He is a wolf after all."

"Yeah, but he isn't taking any of my calls." I replied.

"How convenient," He said snidely.

"We need to move, now. If Jeff had anything to do with this, she would be safe." I paused, thinking then added, "Unless it is his mother, then she is as good as dead. Every minute that we wait, puts her in danger."

Ambrose shook his head, "No, every time you get involved, puts her in danger."

"Shut up Ambrose, you haven't even given me a chance to fight, to see what I am capable of." I replied.

"You—are—weak." He snarled, "I don't need to see what you are capable of. You have not killed enough to be able to do what needs to be done! You are also a liability," he turned to face Erick and pointed, "just like him. The only reason I'm here—is to tell you, not to get in my way." He replied.

"I'm sorry—are you the lone ranger suddenly?" I scoffed. "Need I remind you that she is not your daughter!" I shouted, stood and moved swiftly towards him. "You have no control over me or her. I will do whatever I have to do to get her back!" He came at me with full force, tearing at my flesh and pinning me against the wall. I felt absolutely powerless. I tried to fight back but his control over my mind kept me defenceless. I fought against him as hard as I could. Pushing against him with full force but nothing worked. I started to cry and he let me go.

"You are not ready." He growled through clenched teeth. He turned away. "You're pathetic!"

"I hate you!" I screamed and shoved him away from me.

He chuckled, "You are weak and useless!" He taunted. The anger in him was something I had not seen in a long time. "I know that I am not her father, you don't need to constantly remind of that. But I love her like she was mine and I want to make sure we get her back— alive." He stressed.

"I don't want your help." I shouted shoving him again.

"You need me," He scoffed. My heart raced and I did not know what to do with myself.

"No I don't."

"You need me!" he repeated.

"I just proved it. You can't even fight me, and I'm not as strong as some of the others." He shrugged. "The last thing that I will do for you is train you to fight."

"No!" I walked away. "Erick can train me."

"No, Erick cannot. He is no longer of use to you Sarah. He is human like you once were. How strong were you then?" he stated. "I can train you." He followed me around the table.

"I don't want you here! It was bad enough you invaded my life, ruining everything."

"You know—I'm sick and tired of your whining!" He shoved his face in mine. "You don't get a say anymore." He replied and grabbed my glass. I watched as he filled the glass again then handed it to me. "This only lasts for so long. If you want to be strong you need to feed, on a live donor." He replied. "You need to take a life and replenish every inch of your body. You will never know what you are capable of until you succeed at that." I rolled my eyes at him. Erick finished eating and walked over to the sink to clean his dish. "Erick is a perfect donor." He turned around in Erick's direction just in time to see the surprised look on his face.

"No, he can't heal anymo—"

Erick interjected, "Sarah!" He spun around his brows furrowed.

I shrugged, "I did not realize it was a secret."

Erick shook his head at me.

"That is not the point." He said in disbelief.

"So—what can you do, Angel boy—anything?" Ambrose asked rudely.

"I can be her live donor." He turned away from the both of us.

"Once a day angel boy," Ambrose added. "If she is training, it could be twice a day."

"Fine—whatever she needs," He replied. I could see his knuckles were white from clenching the counter.

"No! I'm not going to make him do that!" I replied stepping in front of Ambrose. "I don't want to wait! I want to go get her now. I don't even care if I die—"

"Sarah!" Erick gasped.

"Well I don't, just as long as she is safe." I was so frustrated and tired of saying this over and over again. "I don't even care if you are the one to take care of her Ambrose, just get her back!" I screamed. He shook his head at me and walked away.

Then he craned his head to look back to me and said, "Starting tomorrow we train. One week, if you are not ready, I leave without you." He started to walk out of the kitchen. He turned to face Erick, "and if you are weak from feeding Erick, find a replacement that can be disposed of." And then he was gone. I threw the closest thing to me, at the door he exited. I looked at Erick who just stood there staring.

"What?"

"Clean it up." He turned and walked away.

"You don't have to do this Erick—we could just kill him." I went after him. I grabbed his arm forcing him to stop.

Erick turned around laughing, "Do you honestly think it will be easy to just dispose of Ambrose?" He stared at me. "He is five hundred years old Sarah. He knows a few tricks." He stated then walked out.

"I don't want to work with him. I don't even want to be in the same room with him Erick." I hollered as he turned the corner. I followed him down the hall.

"He has a way in Sarah. There are no other choices. I am defenceless. I can only do so much." He said so coldly.

"That is not true. You don't know what you can or can't do."

"But I cannot risk waiting to see what I am capable of." His eyes bored into mine, "It's too risky Sarah, we need him and that is final."

"Erick—"

"I can be your blood supply. Keep you strong." He said.

"No!" I didn't get a chance to argue Erick beamed out of the room. I threw the picture frame that was on the vanity table at the white orbs while screaming at him. I really hated that the men in my life could just disappear and reappear whenever they wanted. I grabbed my cell phone and walked outside.

I dialled Jeff's number again. There was no answer. I debated on leaving a message but hung up before the answering machine finished its message. Hesitating momentarily, as I entered the house, walking straight to my room and locked the door. It would not stop either of them from entering but at least they would know I did not want to be disturbed. With my eyes closed and concentration on my breathing eventually led me into a deep sleep.

Chapter Two

The dream I had was dark and creepy. The room was so cold that I could see my own breath. I tried to call out but there was no sound that left my lips. I walked around aimlessly in the darkness searching for any sign of life. Then it became hot and it felt as though my skin was melting off my bones. I opened my eyes to find Erick was standing by the fireplace. I sat up and watched him for a moment. Then he turned around to face me. Beads of sweat covered my forehead and chest.

"I believe I locked the door." I scowled.

"Like that has ever stopped me." He laughed.

"Good to see you're in a better mood." I rolled my eyes and laid back. It went quiet for a few minutes.

Erick cleared his throat, "Thought a fire would be good."

"Are you cold?" I asked.

"No, but once you are done—"

I interjected, "I am not drinking from you—"

"Yes you are and you will. Every night from this day forward, until we leave." He walked over to the bed pulling off his shirt. "Alaina needs you to be as strong as you are built to be."

"I don't even know how to be strong anymore." I covered my face with my hand.

"You do be fine." He sat on the edge of the bed.

"You are not coming with us." I said sternly, trying not to look up at him.

But, my hormones got the best of me and my eyes scanned over his body like an x-ray machine. I licked my lips as I watched the blood flow through his veins. He made things worse by having his shirt off. I gulped and shut my eyes tight like a child pretending to sleep when her parents peek on her. Then he cupped my face.

I turned away because my fangs protruded the gums the instant his skin touched mine. I pushed his hand away.

Breathlessly I said, "I don't want you to do this."

"I know." He leaned in real slow then kissed my cheek and my nose then chin. I tried to move away but the headboard was there. He sat back slightly and just looked at me. I searched for an escape. "You won't hurt me." He whispered his fingers gently touching my lips.

I shook my head fighting the tears, "I could kill you." I whispered.

"I trust you." He replied. "Besides, Ambrose is here if anything should go wrong." I sighed and rolled my eyes.

"Why?" I shuffled away but Erick grabbed me and pulled me to him. My back was against his chest. His lips touched my ear. My entire body froze. I could feel the burning sensation between my legs take hold of me and I tried everything to control it. Then I felt his hands under my shirt, slowly sliding their way up gasped as his hands cupped my breasts. I bit my lip and tried so hard to contain my desire for a little while longer but Erick would not stop. He playfully bit down on my neck awakening something inside me I forgot was there. Something I wanted to forget.

Ambrose walked towards the bed. His eyes locked on mine. My eyes told him to come closer but my mind was aware that he was coming for me. I closed my eyes and tried to pretend he was leaving. Then his fingers touched my cheek. His thumb brushed across my bottom lip. My entire body quivered at his touch and I was even more aroused than a moment ago. I bit down playfully on his thumb. His lips parted, letting out a gasp. His hand cupped my cheek. Just as he was about to move in to kiss me, I held my hand on his chest shaking my head and smiling. I turned away from him, grabbed Erick and pinned him down on the bed kissing him aggressively. With one free hand, I unbuttoned his pants and slid my hand in. My lips made their way down his neck to his chest, my tongue traced along his lean muscular, tanned body. Pleasure filled me as I listened to him moan. My panties wet with desire. Erick's arms wrapped around me but I had to I gently pulled away. I got off the bed, lifted my nightshirt over my head then wiggled out of my panties. Hungrily their eyes watched me. Erick was on the bed waiting. Ambrose stood next to me, wanting so much to take me.

Ambrose licked his lips. Erick's heart raced and I could hear every beat in my head. I stood there before them completely naked now, waiting for someone to take the next step but neither of them moved. I couldn't wait. If I stood here any longer, my senses would catch up to me and I would tell them to leave. I made my way around the bed towards Ambrose. My head titled slightly and I playfully bit down on my finger. In my head, I knew I would regret this but it felt like someone had taken over my body. The desire to sleep with them both was strong. The thought of having them inside me excited me. Drinking their blood pulled me out of my sanity.

"You want me?" I whispered breathlessly. I reached out and touched his hand. His lip trembled but he held his composure. He probably sense I wouldn't go through with it. I didn't know if I would go through with it but the heat of the moment was guiding me and I was enjoying it.

"Sarah—" Erick moaned distracting me a little.

"Yes?" I hissed never taking my eyes off Ambrose.

My fingers began to unbutton Ambrose's shirt. His eyes focused on mine. "Do you want me?" I asked. He didn't answer. I turned my head in a way so that I could expose my neck to Ambrose. Erick crawled across the bed towards me and knelt at the edge. That was when I felt Ambrose's kiss on my neck. I whimpered and pulled him tight against my body. My head jerked back to look at him. He kissed my cheek then pulled away averting his eyes. I stared him down waiting for him to look up at me. Erick now stood behind me, his arms wrapped around my waist. So many naughty thoughts were going through my mind right now. I unbutton the last button on Ambrose's shirt and slid it off his shoulders. Then I leaned forward and kissed his bare chest.

"Sarah." Erick whispered. "Leave him be."

"He wants to join us Erick," I replied. I traced my hands down Ambrose's chest to his pants.

"Sarah." Erick said pulling me away.

"You have no idea what it feels like, being this close to him right now." I said gaspingly. "We can feel everything." I stared into Ambrose's eyes. "He is very aroused right now. I can feel it and—I kind of want him too." I moved in close but he stopped me. I reached up to touch his face and he stopped me again. I stood naked in front of him and he was avoiding me now. His restraint was very good considering his mind was racing with thoughts of what he wanted to do to me.

"Sarah." Erick said disappointedly.

"Shush." I unbuttoned Ambrose's pants. I kept my eyes on his. He was acting tough, as if what I was doing did not affect him. I slid my fingers around his neck, pulled him in and kissed him. He kissed me back this time but he still tried to pull away. His eyes were heavy and his chest was moving faster now. I was breaking him down slowly. I grabbed his arms and placed them around my waist. I kissed him again but he stopped me. I watched as he studied me. His eyes very focused. Then his eyes shifted and he looked over at Erick who was patiently waiting for this little game to end. My thoughts must have wandered because a sneer formed across Ambrose's face then he leaned in real close, his eyes still on mine and said, "Fuck you."

"That's the plan." I chuckled. He turned and walked away. I watched as he left the room. "What's gotten into him?" I sighed. When I turned back to Erick, he was getting dressed. I walked towards him. I swear being a vampire made sex more complicated than it needed to be. The other thing was that it did not matter, as a vampire, that I was angry with Erick. The moment I smelt him and heard his blood pulsating through his veins, I wanted him in whichever way I could get him. The hardest part was fighting it. He wanted it too and I could smell his need to have me but because I did what I did with Ambrose, he was no longer in the mood. I took his hand in mine just after he put his shirt back on. His jaw tightened. He stood there silent for a long time. I reached out to touch him.

"Stay." I whispered. He shook his head and started to walk away. "I'm sorry."

"You are sorry a lot lately Sarah."

"Don't you dare go there Erick!" I growled. I never gave him a chance to retaliate, "You are the one who locked me in a cellar for God knows how long, with Ambrose's help, I might add. I should be furious with the both of you! But instead I am here willing to be with the both of you, which is totally out of character for me and you practically slap me across the face." I screamed. I stomped across the room to where my nightshirt was on the floor and slipped it over my head then walked towards the door. Erick followed me. He then stood in the doorway just staring at me. "Just get out." I snarled slamming the door shut as he left. In a huff I crawled into bed and pulled the covers up to my head.

It was a little over an hour later he returned. He opened the door and came in. The amber glow of the fire flickered on his human flesh as he slowly walked across the hardwood floor. He crawled across the bed towards me, planting his hands firmly on either side of my body with his legs straddling my waist. The longer curls on his forehead fell forward slightly. His eyes bore into mine. "I did not mean to upset you. I was just—not expecting this sort of . . . arrangement between us." He said.

"Neither did I," I replied.

He bent down and kissed me. His lips were soft and moist. Kissing him was like seeing real magic for the first time.

"I love you." He whispered breathlessly. I wanted to tell him I loved him too but I couldn't. "I brought someone with me." He looked over his shoulder.

Ambrose stood by the fireplace avoiding looking at me. I smirked, feeling no longer in the mood after earlier. "In case I am too tired after—you feed."

"Let's not discuss that, okay." I begged grabbing his face so that he looked at me. My hands dropped at my sides and I sat up. "Ambrose." I whispered. His head jerked up and he looked at me. I nodded him over.

His eyes were heavy as he stared down at me. I knelt on the bed to kiss him. His fingers tangled in my hair. He pulled my nightshirt over my head dropping it to the floor. His hands were on my skin again. He leaned forward forcing me to lay back, Erick on the other side of the bed watching. They took turns kissing me. The three of us enjoyed each other immensely.

When I felt the lust for blood kick in I pulled Erick close, slowly bringing my lips to his neck, giving it a quick kiss then I bit down and let the coppery sweet nectar of the Gods fill my pallet. When I opened my eyes to look at him, I noticed him wince and gasped in pain but then he laced his fingers with mine. Reminding me of who I was, giving me the power to stop. I pulled away from him to see that his eyes were glossy. Mine now replenished with his blood. I licked my lips then kissed him. His head fell back effortlessly on the pillow, his lips curved in a smile. His arms wrapped around me loosely. Immortality was so complicated. I could still feel Ambrose around me. Erick's eyes closed as the weakness took over. I rested my head on his chest and cried. Ambrose lied down beside me. His index finger tickled at my side.

"Are you all right?" He asked. I nodded and tried to speak but sobs came out. "You don't look fine." His hand loosely cupped my face. Staring into his feral grey eyes brought me back to reality again. I would never be able to take this moment back. The evil monster that hides inside of me was let loose and I did something I know I will regret for the rest of my life. I drank from Erick and I slept with the enemy again. I continued to weep, covering my face with my hands. I was embarrassed and I should be.

What kind of person had I become?

"Don't be ridiculous. Think of it this way, it wasn't with two complete strangers and no one died." He pulled me to him. "This is who you are now. This is what we do and if you think that it is all sparkles and candy kisses you are sorely mistaken." Just like Ambrose to tell it like it is. He got of the bed, because just as it was like Ambrose to tell it like it is, he hated to hear it himself. I watched him dress and leave the room. He loathed himself as much I did.

Chapter Three

'Waaaake uuuup . . .' A whisper filled my head.

I sat straight up, looked around the room to find Ambrose standing there. Shame filled me to the very core even when I opened my eyes again. He must have been the one whispering my name the entire time. He is playing games with me.

"You are the one playing mind games again." He snarled turning towards me.

"Really, that's funny considering I'm the one hearing voices and having strange dreams, vivid as they were before I became this monster!" I ripped the comforter off.

"I have no idea what you are talking about." He replied his tone very annoyed.

"Someone keeps whispering my name. I now know it's you." I replied and hopped out of bed. Ambrose back to business as usual.

"If you are hearing voices in your head Sarah, maybe it's time you see a shrink." He turned towards the door.

"What do you want Ambrose?" I asked standing beside him with my arms crossed.

"What I want for you to do is get dressed." He glanced away.

"I'm sorry does my nakedness bother you? You seemed fine with it last night."

"Just—get dressed and come downstairs." He said.

"What for, more humiliation?" I snapped.

"No one is humiliating you Sarah you do that all on your own." He hissed.

"Screw you Ambrose." I leapt to my feet.

"I believe you already have." He snapped then left the room slamming the door behind him.

I grabbed the house coat on the door and stormed out after him. But every corner he turned, with great speed. When I entered the kitchen, they were both standing there waiting. I glared at both of them and sat down. Erick handed me a glass filled with blood.

"What?" I asked waiting in anticipation for what they were going to throw at me next.

"We've just found out some information that may be of some use to us." He said. I stared him down waiting for him to continue. "The wolves that have Alaina, are in Connecticut," he added.

"Are you kidding me?" I stood and the chair practically crashed as his skid across the floor.

"No and you are not coming." Ambrose replied walking towards me, "Don't look at me like that. You're not ready." He took my glass and poured me another. "I promise when I find her, I will bring her here."

"What if you don't find her?" I asked.

"I will do everything I can, to find her." Ambrose replied. His eyes locked on mine, inside I believed him but I didn't want him to be the one to save her. Giving Ambrose the upper hand was not in the game plan.

"I am going with you, whether you like it or not!" I stood in front of him. "She is my daughter—not yours and no matter what you say I will go where ever I have to, to fight for her." Through all the arguing Erick said nothing. He stared at the table and strummed his fingers. Ambrose paid no mind to him and continued to debate with me.

Then foolishly, I let myself into Erick's head. What a big mistake that was. All I could hear were a cluster of thoughts. I could not make sense out of any of it. He loved me so much but felt it would never be anything more than what we shared the other night. He was crying inside and while arguing with Ambrose, Erick's feelings began to fester in me. Then the room fell silent. I had not noticed that they were both staring at me and I was staring at Erick. My cheeks flushed as his thoughts of last night flashed in my mind.

"What?" I gulped knowing I was busted.

Erick glowered at me, "How dare you!" He stood up. "Those are my thoughts!"

"Wha—how—oh—like that ever stopped you from getting in my head!" I shouted. I sounded very much like a child but this was becoming more tedious as time went on.

"When you asked me to stop, I did." He replied. "Besides, that is not the point."

"Then what is your point Erick?" I replied. The look on Erick's face horrified me. I had never seen him so angry.

"Let's get ready to leave shall we." He said and stormed out of the room.

"Shit." I ran my fingers through my curly hair. Ambrose chuckled. "Do you enjoy other people's misery?"

"Just yours," He chortled.

"Go to hell."

"Already there," He laughed and started for the door.

"When did this become a fucking soap opera?" I shouted and threw a glass at him but it hit the wall and shattered across the floor. I screamed in frustration then turned and walked towards the patio door. It shattered under my touch. I looked down at my hands surprised. That was something new. My powers seem to react when I am angry. I will have to remember that when I am cornered with Ambrose again. I smiled widely. This was taking too long I needed to find my daughter and now. If Chase were here, we would have already found Alaina.

I stood in the courtyard my head up and I concentrated on her, reaching out to her with my mind. Finding her was my only mission. I walked down the long gravel driveway.

"Hey." Erick startled me. I am a vampire now, how can I still get startled. I stuffed my hands in the pockets of the house coat.

"Hey." I winced.

"Sorry about earlier, I overreacted." He said.

"Why the sudden change of heart Erick. You were pretty pissed off in there." I asked.

"Life is too short to be angry." He tossed a duffle bag on the ground next to me. It landed on the ground with a clank.

"What's that?" I asked walking towards him. I knelt next to the bag unzipped it and gasped. "Seriously?" The bag had weapons of all kinds.

"We can never be too prepared?" He replied shutting the trunk of the car that Ambrose just pulled in.

"Are you planning a war?" I replied grabbing his arm forcing him to look at me.

"No, but one is waiting for us."

"How do you know that?" I asked.

"Your vision," he replied.

"My vision," I ransacked my brain, trying to remember what vision he was talking about when it all came back to me. I stumbled backwards as the faces flash before my eyes. "No," I cried. "No—that can't happen." No other words spoken between us.

Then Ambrose hollered impatiently. "You ladies ready?" He leaned over the hood of the car. "Give me five minutes." I said and ran back to the house. Once I was dressed which took me less than five minutes I rejoined them outside. We all climbed in. I took the backseat.

The drive back to Connecticut brought back so many memories, ones I wish I had forgotten. Thing about being a vampire, you never forget anything. Everything that ever happened to you is as fresh in your mind as the day it happened. We drove past the dorm house that I lived in with Jeff, Liz and Suzie; the field behind the house, where Chase first told me what he was. Further down the road was the old café where I spent many late nights studying, with my friends. The same place where I had first saw Erick in the corner booth. I quickly wiped my face, before the guys saw me crying. It felt so long ago that I was happy here, living a normal life. No one was trying to kill me. I had a family and friends, people who actually cared about me.

"We all care about you Sarah." Erick whispered.

"There you go again invading my thoughts." I scoffed. He chuckled and apologised. The car was silent again. "Stop!" Ambrose was startled when I shouted.

"What?" The car swerved slightly, Ambrose glanced back at me. He did not say another word as he pulled over to the side of the road by the pier. The moment he stopped, I opened the door and got out. I stared out at the calm waters. This was the place where Chase and I first talked about what was really going on in our lives. The bridge; where I told Chase about Zadkiel and how he had bitten me. My hand ran along the railing as I remembered. It was so hard to imagine I would never see him again. My heart ached at the thought of what he went through to protect me.

"We are not here to go down memory lane Sarah." Ambrose said walking up behind me. I wiped my face with both hands then turned around rolling my eyes at him. He watched me make my way back to the car. Erick leaned back on the door with his ankles crossed and hands in his pockets. I shook my head trying to laugh it off but the trembling of my lips made it impossible to hide the sadness that filled my soul. Erick took a step forward to embrace me. I felt his lips on my skin that was when I broke down.

"I'm sorry." He whispered hugging me tight.

"I can't be here." I sobbed. His thumbs wiped the tears that fell. He nodded, kissed my forehead and then pulled me to his chest.

"I know." He whispered. His voice soothed me.

"Clocks ticking," Ambrose said banging the roof of his car. I glared at him but he turned away then slammed the door shut as he got back in the car. I shook my head annoyed and climbed in the back seat again. I curled against the window resting my head on my hand. Erick had turned to face me, his arm over the seat to hold my hand. The sorrow I felt was over whelming and I wanted to scream. Erick's abundance of comfort held me together as we drove through the city. I took my phone out of my pocket and tried Jeff's again. This time a woman answered.

"Hello." She answered.

"May I speak with Jeff please?" I asked.

"No you may not—" there was a scuffle, some words said.

"Hello?" The male voice took over.

"Jeff?" I said anxiously.

"No—uh this is his brother. May I ask who is calling?"

I covered the mouthpiece on the phone. "Brother?"

"Sarah?" The male voice came through loudly.

"How do you know my name?" I asked.

Ambrose pulled over.

"Hang up the phone!" He turned to look at me.

"Jeff told me all about you." He answered. Something was not right. I knew Jeff, he never ever mentioned a brother. He distinctly told me he was an only child.

"Where is Jeff?"

"Hang up the phone Sarah," Ambrose said again, "it's not Jeff or his family!"

"Jeff's dead."

"What?" I gasped and dropped the phone. Erick opened his door and got in the backseat with me. He picked up the phone and spoke. Ambrose was watching me through the mirror. I listened to Erick but none of the words made any sense. I was rambling to myself and Ambrose was getting really annoyed.

"Sarah!" He shouted. "Pull yourself together!"

"Jeff doesn't have a brother, he is an only child." I said softly as I remembered. "No—he is lying." I blurted. "Jeff doesn't have a brother!" I started to scream frantically. I threw the phone out the window. "Sarah, calm yourself!" Erick said. I jumped out of the car.

"Jeff doesn't have a brother."

"What the hell are you talking about?" Ambrose replied following suit.

"I knew him for five years Ambrose. He told me he was an only child." I replied.

"So who could that of been?" Erick asked.

"I don't know, one of them?" I shrugged. "He said Jeff is dead. That would be the only reason he never answered any of my calls." I paced running my fingers through my hair. "There is no way to know for sure. Unless we were to go to his parent's house," I said.

"Where does he live?"

"I don't know somewhere upstate. They are rich and they are werewolves." I replied.

"Somewhere secluded," Ambrose stated.

"Okay where?"

"Hamptons." Erick suggested.

"Well then, we'll need a new plan." Ambrose said and walked away.

"What do you mean a new plan?"

"Well were's have a keen sense of smell, they can spot a vampire miles away." He replied.

"So what do we do then?"

"We find humans and send them in."

"Are you crazy? We can't do that to innocent people!" I scowled.

"Innocent? There is no such thing and yes, we can. I have many familiars that would do it, besides I pay well." He stated. I tried to protest but he cut me off. "Spare me your 'we can't hurt the humans' speech. I don't care remember and I hurt people all the time." He gave a smug smile then walked away.

"Don't you ever get tired of these games?" I scowled.

"That's life Chère, get used to it."

"Ambrose, we are not the same. My life will never end up as yours did." I scowled.

"We shall see." He hissed then tugged at a strand of hair.

"You disgust me. How can you live your life like this? Don't you care about anything but yourself?"

"Care!" He shouted and came at me like a bat outta hell, "All I have done since I fuckin' met you is care!" Spit sprayed out of his mouth. "You think I enjoy feeling this way!" He held me by the throat. I turned my head away. "I hate feeling like this," He let me go. He ran his fingers through his shaggy hair.

"Why?"

"Let's just say people that I love tend to die and it's not always my fault." He shouted. "You know what— you're on your own." He walked towards the car but Erick stood in front of him trying to stop him. "Really aAngel boy, what are you gonna do?" He laughed. I touched

Ambrose's shoulder trying to calm him. I attempted an apology but even he knew it wasn't sincere. "Get on with it Sarah." He shrugged my hand off his shoulder.

"Let's go." I sighed and got back in the car. The ride from here on out was uncomfortable.

Chapter Four

We grabbed a motel room against my protests. I sat on the bed tapping my leg with my fingers. Erick stood by the window and Ambrose paced the rooms staring at his phone. Sitting around like a bunch of idiots waiting for something to happen was infuriating me.

"Will you please stop tapping your fingers," Ambrose shouted.

"Oh I'm sorry is this bothering you!" I snapped.

"Just knock it off." He continued to pace.

"Why don't you relax? You're making it tense for everyone with your bloody pacing!" I replied.

"Would you like me to leave you two alone, so you can—you know, handle the sexual tension."

"No!" We both shouted at Erick then looked in opposite directions.

"I don't want to be left alone with this filthy creature." I spat.

"Feelings mutual," Ambrose replied snidely.

"God it's ridiculous how you two act around each other. I can't believe I never noticed it before." He scoffed.

"Don't be ridiculous Erick." I replied standing and walking towards him. I peered out the window ignoring his stare. "What do we do now?" Just then, the phone rang. Ambrose answered halfway through the first ring. Erick and I jumped turning to watch him.

"Hello." He walked into the bathroom. I groaned. Several minutes later, he returned to the room where we waited anxiously.

"Well." I asked as Ambrose came out of the bathroom.

"They are heading in now." Ambrose said hanging up.

"What—I thought you said we would all go." I replied.

"Well I changed my mind." He replied. I screamed and flew at him.

"I can't wait 'til you're out of my life. Better yet, dead, just so I don't have to deal with you anymore!" I screamed.

"Then kill me!" He pushed me away.

Erick opened the door and left.

Neither of us noticed.

"Once they have contact they will call." Ambrose replied.

"What about the part when their heads are ripped off once they realize who they work for huh?" I asked.

"Doesn't matter."

"It does matter!" I shouted flailing my arms about.

"If they die we send in some more until we get the answer we are looking for!"

"You disgust me."

"Yet, you're still here." He chided.

"Not by choice." I scoffed then stood with my arms folded.

"Then leave." He said inching closer. When I turn around, he was in my face. "I won't stop you. Turn around and walk out." He pointed to the door. His lips inches away from mine but I held my ground.

"Mark my words Ambrose, the instant that I'm able to kill you, I will drive a stake through your black heart."

"Bring it sister. Just know this—I will not go down without a fight." He growled. My lip twitched but not from fear, from anger. I meant every word I said. I step away but he followed. Then, he pulled a stake out from his back pocket, pointed it at me and said, "Why not now? Huh? You don't really need me you can find Jeff's house all on your own. Kill me." He held it out to me. "Take it . . . TAKE IT!" He screamed.

"STOP IT!" I begged.

"Put me out of my fuckin' misery please!" he screamed.

"NO!" I shouted back and pushed him away. "I won't!"

"That's because you're weak!" His anger was fierce. "This is why you ruin everything. You cannot defend yourself because you are weak. You're a useless vampire and I don't know why I created you. No one ever made from my blood, acted so pathetically."

"Fuck you!" I screamed and slapped him.

"That's it, get angry." He growled. He continued to bate me, so I hit him again. "DO IT!" He held the stake against my chest. Tears filled my eyes and I picture myself driving the stake through his heart. Then I screamed at him again. Suddenly he grabbed me and kissed me, pinning me against the wall. I did not fight him off, not right away. I wrap my one arm around him, stake still tight in the grasp of my other hand. He lifted me up against the wall pulling down my jeans and undoing his pants. My fangs hurt as they protrude through my gums and lightly graze his neck.

"Why do I want you so bad?" He said kissing me.

"Because you can't have me," I said. Then he gasped and backed away, slowly. He looked down at his chest. I cried. My breathing was heavy. The blood dripped from the stake that I just shoved in his chest. He glanced up at me and his mouth slightly parted, I waited for him to speak but only blood trickled out. He dropped to his knees.

"Weak my ass," I said smugly.

✳✳✳✳✳

Later, when Erick walked through the door, he found me squatting in a corner with my head in my hands and Ambrose with his pants around his ankles, stake in his chest.

"What the hell happened?" Erick asked. "Why are his pants off?"

"He told me to do it."

"Do what, take of his pants or stake him?"

"Kill him." I cried running fingers through my hair. "I hated him Erick."

"I know but why are his pants off," He glared at me. I could not look up at him. "You're right. I shouldn't be here." He knelt with one knee on Ambrose's chest and pulled the stake out then handed it back to me. "You'll need that to protect yourself." He stormed out the glass shaking as the door slammed.

I got off the floor and sat on the bed, nervously tapping my blood stained fingers on my thigh. With the cell phone in my other hand and Ambrose's body lying lifeless on the floor. Blood soiled the carpet and I did not know what to do or whom I was to call to fix this.

Ambrose was right I did ruin things. I screwed everything up by not thinking anything through first. It was close to midnight and I was thirsting pretty badly.

Erick had not returned. Then the phone rang.

"Hello—" Just then, Ambrose leapt from the ground and grabbed me by the throat, slapping the phone out of my hand. "Ambrose." I gasped. Tears filled my eyes and for the first time, I really feared for my life. The grip on my throat was tight and I could feel my larynx cracking under the pressure.

"You want to feel pain?" He screamed and snapped my neck. "I'll fuckin' show you pain!" He cried. My body slumped to the floor and Ambrose dropped like a sack of potatoes beside me.

*****

Several hours had passed . . . .

I sat straight up gasping for air. I clenched and clawed at my throat as it slowly healed. My eyes shot towards Ambrose who sat on the armchair with his head in his hands. I could not move. I let my body relax and leaned back against the bed, tears pouring down my face.

"Why are you still here?" I asked my voice hoarse. He tossed me a bag of blood.

"I don't know," He scoffed. Then he wiped his face with one hand.

"What's happened?" My voice cracked.

"The council went in and took her. The pack is all dead. If Jeff was there, most likely he is dead too."

"What?" Was all I could muster up. The pain in my throat was unbearable.

"My human arrived just after the take down. He saw most of what happened."

"Wh—"

"Just stop." He finally looked up at me. His eyes bore into mine. I did not need his thoughts to seep in. I could see it written all over his face. His cheeks stained with bloody tears. "You go back to Erick and—and I will go anywhere you're not." He pushed himself up from his thighs.

"Wait a minute." I held my throat. Ambrose cut his wrist and offered it to me, but I refuse.

"You want to be able to talk and finish the healing then drink." My lips touched his wound before it healed shut again. I wiped the blood from my mouth on my jacket sleeve then swallowed a few times before trying to speak. My voice was slightly better and it hurt less.

"Why would you leave now? You have been fighting with me for so long." I knelt beside him.

"You're right."

"I am?"

"I'm not her father and you hate me. Besides, you have already tried to kill me once." He stood up. "I don't need this shit. My life was less complicated before I met you."

"I don't believe that! As if a little complication would stop you. What is your real reason Ambrose?"

"You want the truth Sarah?" He paused, I glanced away and he laughed, "That's right, you already know it." He walked towards me and I looked up at him. I gulped painfully, even though I knew this already. "I love you." His voice trailed off. "I don't want to, but I do."

"I made it clear from the start, my feelings towards you. How can you still love me? I have never been nice to you. There must be someone other than me that you love." I asked.

"The last woman that I really truly loved, more than myself, was my wife. But she died a long time ago." His voice trailed off then he started for the door.

"Please don't tell me I look like her!" I winced.

"Not even close. She was the most beautiful woman I had ever laid eyes on." He replied harshly.

"Ah—ouch." I replied.

"I don't mean it that way." He turned to face me. "You're beautiful Sarah. You know you are. My wife was the most beautiful soul in the entire world." His eyes welled. "Anyway . . . ever since I met you, my life has been turned upside down and I can't deal with it anymore."

"I did nothing to make any of that happen. I told you I wanted nothing to do with you. You knew I was in love with Chase, if you fell in love me it is of your own doing."

"I don't argue that." He laughed half-heartedly. "Thing is, no man needs you to do anything to fall in love with you. They just fall in love with you. You're a plague Sarah." He scowled.

"Excuse me." I retorted feeling a pang in my chest. No one had ever used words to hurt me the way Ambrose does.

"You slowly destroy the lives of men." He replied.

I stood with my hands on my hips. "You're being ridiculous."

"Am I?" He replied angrily. "I want you, but I can't have you—well not all of you." He sneered then turned his back to me and stared out the window. "Sure, there has been plenty that I have wanted but if I wanted it, I took it. I never asked their permission. You're the first thing that I have come across in my five hundred years that I cannot have and am afraid to take." He explained, "That is why you are a plague. Men love you, without even knowing it and then it's too late." He sighed, "We stupid fools are drawn to you like moths to a flame. You will be the death of us all." His lips pressed tight.

My eyes watered, "Death of you all? That's a bit dramatic Ambrose, even for you." I said.

He slowly craned his neck to look at me his eyes filled with pain. "Started with Jeff didn't it? Then Chase now Erick, no doubt eventually me. We all love you and all of us have or will die, for you." The light from the window glistened off his wet cheek.

"That's not fair." My voice broke. "I never asked for any of this. I never did anything different than before and I most certainly didn't want anyone to die."

"Your right, you never asked for any of it, but it happened. Just like the plague. It sweeps in under our noses and leaves us dead in the night." His lips trembled. His hand squeezed the doorknob. He knew I would never want him or love him. He terrified me from the moment he came into my life. He threatened to kill me so many times, how could he possibly think I would eventually fall in love with him. I stood there speechless with my mouth gaping as Ambrose walked out, this may in fact be the last time I see him.

      'You did this to yourself.' I cried out to him.

      'Perhaps,' He replied. *'Now I can undo it.'* That was the last thing I heard him say before I felt completely shut out from his mind.

Chapter Five

I was alone for the first time in a long time. Even though it made it easier to get around, I missed the constant banter that occupied my thoughts. The sun was at its first sign of setting. I walked the shoreline, along the homes of Hamptons most prestigious, while they dined. I could smell the blood pulsating through their veins as they went about their daily lives oblivious to the dangers that walk outside the doors.

My mind wandered as I continued to walk. I began to sniff out any scent left of Alaina. Then it happened, it was faint but it was her scent, so I follow it. Running felt good after being stuck in a car for so long. I ran until I reached the house where the scent was the strongest. Slowly, I walk the compounds of the lot, not a soul in sight. If they could sniff out a vampire from a mere mile away, they were losing their touch.

When I reached the house I tried the front door, it was already open slightly. Gently pushing the door open the rest of the way, I walked in. The smell of fresh blood and death hovered in the air. My mouth watered and my fangs began to protrude. No sign of a body yet but the stench became stronger the farther I walked through the house. With my back up against the wall, I slowly push the door open to the kitchen with my booted foot. The sight before me was unbearable. There were torn limbs scattered throughout the room. Blood covered the ceramic tiles, splattered the walls and ceiling. I cover my mouth from the stench. Tears well in my eyes, then I saw him.

"No!" I gasped falling to my knees and pulling him onto my lap. There was black liquid seeping out of his wounds. When I touch it, it shimmered on my fingertips. "Silver?" I said to myself, "Oh Jeff, I'm so sorry."

"Are ye now?" Someone with a Scottish accent from behind me replied. I craned my neck to look up at the man hovering over me. I jumped to my feet and spun around charging at him. My teeth barred ready to rip open his neck. "Whoa! Relax love, I'm no here tae figh'." He said but I didn't believe him. Trusting anyone right now was not something I could do.

"Are you Ambrose's lackey?" I asked. He shook his head.

"I take it ye ken the lad?" I stared at him confused. "You know him." He says putting on an American accent.

"You're pretty observant." I hissed keeping him pinned with my forearm.

"Wha' happened?"

"What you don't know?" I replied a little surprised. "You weren't hiding out 'til they were all dead?"

"I've only just arrived love. I was tae come here for the wee lass." He looked around the room.

"Lass," I asked standing erect.

"Yeah, the little girl," He chuckled.

"Yeah I understand what Lass means. Why are you here for her?" I let him go and cross my arms.

"Wait a minute, who did ye say ye were?"

"I didn't." I replied and started for the door.

"You're her aren't ye?" He smiled excitedly.

"Who's her?" I replied callously and continued to walk through the house with him at my heel. I needed to get away from him. I did not like the fact that he was looking for my daughter.

"The mother," He said.

My body went numb and I wanted to spin around and attack him but I could not move at all. How did he know so much about me?

"I'm nae here tae hurt ye."

"That's what they all say." I scowled then leapt for his throat. He was strong though. He flung me off and I hit the wall across the room. I jumped to my feet breathlessly. When I got up and tried to go after him again he held me back without touching me.

"I believe we have come off tae a bad start." He said. "The names Lennox," he held out his hand and I chuckled. "And like I said I'm nae here tae hurt ye."

"I really don't care!" I said and went for his neck again. He pins me against the wall again. "How are you doing that? Are you a demon?" I gasped.

"Ye dinnae ken your mythology tae well do ye." He laughed. "Look lass, I wulnae let ye go if ye dinnae cam doon!" He groans. He was pressing hard against my diaphragm so that I couldn't breathe. "I dinnae believe, wha' they plan tae dae wi' yer daughter is reit. I'm nae fur it."

"What do they want to do with my daughter?" I asked.

"Ah—sae ye ur the mother." He smiled.

"What do they want with her?" I demanded.

"I dunno, clone her."

"What?"

"I dunno whit they plan tae dae wi' 'er. All I ken is once they have what they need, she wulnae be any use tae them." He replied.

"How do you know all of this?" I asked.

"I just do." Was all he said.

"How do I know you are not lying to me?" I walked towards him but he lifted his hand and I stopped.

"I have nae leverage here, so why would I lie? I want tae help ye fin' her too." He said as sincerely as he could.

"Why, so you can take her to whoever hired you?" I scowled.

"I guess ye will just have tae trust me."

"Good luck with that." I replied. I walked towards the back door. "By the way, people tend to die around me. Just sayin'," I stated.

"Good to know." He said glancing back.

Together we walked through the back of the house straight into the forest. I could not have any one see us leave that place. It was best to let them believe we were part of the pile of bodies.

"So, who would have done that?" I asked once we were far enough away.

"The council," He replied all too quickly.

"Seriously?" I replied.

"That is their trademark. When anyone finds a massacre ay 'at magnitude, it means they want us aw tae ken 'at they mean business"

After piecing what he said all together I replied. "Great."

"I'm sorry abit your mate. Did ye ken him well?"

"He was Alaina's father." I continued walking.

"Och that's too bad." He said. Thankfully the rest of the walk was silent. When we reached a main road, I stopped and turned to face him.

"Well." I placed my hands on my hips.

"What now?" He asked lighting a cigarette.

"We part ways." I said and started walking away from him.

"What're ye talkin' abit? I said I wanted tae help." Lennox replied.

"I don't want your help." I replied.

"Ye ken fur a vampire you're pretty stupid." He laughs and folds his arms across his chest.

"You know for a guy, you're really annoying?" I mocked.

"Och—sae ye have a sense of humour. I'm impressed." He laughed. "Goin' against the council, is a death sentence an' ye cannae dae it alone."

"I'm quite aware of that." I folded my arms and rested against my one foot. "We have a history, the council and I. They interfered in my life, one too many times."

"Ah see." He replied.

"I really don't want to be standing here telling you my life story, so if you don't mind, I'd like to be alone." I walked away.

"I'm sure ye dae. But—I can be ay use tae ye."

"What part of I don't trust you or anything you have to say, don't you understand." I asked then turned to walk away.

"Gezz a chance hen, all right." He holds his arms up as if to say, come on.

I shook my head and said, "I swear to god, if you so much as rub me the wrong way, I'll kill you."

"Sure lass." He laughed shaking his head. I turned away annoyed. It was going be a long journey. I tossed my phone so that Erick or Ambrose could not contact me. I'm sure I was the last thing on their minds right now anyway.

"I need to make a quick stop." I said spotting a store across the street. I spend the last few dollars in my wallet on new clothes from head to toe. When I came out Lennox was shocked.

"Whit happened tae the bonnie lassie Ah saw go in there?" He laughed.

"She's dead." I replied slipping the leather motor cycle jacket over my shoulders and zipping it up.

"Well, Ah hae tae say, it looks good on ye." He smiled.

"Your opinion doesn't matter. It's practical and leather tends to stop certain objects better than cotton." I rolled my eyes at him. Why was I explaining myself to him? If I wanted to dress in all leather, that was my choice.

"Ah meant nae offense love."

"Stop calling me that." I said and walked ahead of him.

Chapter Six

We stopped at a motel for the night. As it turned out, Lennox was a great deal of help after all. Apparently, his Intel on what happened to Alaina was more useful than any information I got from Ambrose. Speaking of Ambrose, I was quite surprised they had not tracked me down. Lennox pitched in for the motel. Unfortunately, my money was still stashed back at the house, on the Coffman's Isle.

"I need a favour." I said walking out of the bathroom after my shower. He watched me as I dried my hair with the towel.

Lennox smiled, "Anither," then sat back in his chair.

"I've asked for a favour prior to this one?" I replied, my fingers pressed at my temple. "Jog my memory please."

"What's the favour Lass?" He leaned forward on his knees.

"I have money stashed at my house but I can't go back there. Can you get in and out without alerting anyone there?" I asked.

"Possibly . . . where is this house?"

"That island just off the coast of Connecticut."

"Are ye kiddin' me?" He turned around.

I shook my head. "The money will get us where we need to go."

"And where is 'at?" He replied leaning forward.

"Europe."

"Have ye lost your min'? We cannae go there without a bloody army." Lennox scoffed. "You're insane."

"You don't have to come." I replied callously.

"Reit, like I'll send ye tae the lion's den on yur ain."

"I'm used to it."

"I dinnae care if ur use tae it or no', that's no' how Ah work." He shook his head and packed his things up. "Where's this place I need tae go." I gave him the directions. "Ye ken if ah ken yur name I would stop calling ye lass." He winked.

"I'm not here to be friends. You are the one who wanted to tag along, remember." I replied walking away.

"Suit yursel'." He cleared his throat and hauled the bag over his shoulder. "See ye in a wee while."

"Sarah." I replied rolling my eyes at him, he turned to look at me smiling.

"I'll see ye soon . . . Sarah." He said then left.

*****

I paced the room for hours, hoping he makes it there and back in one piece. There is a knock at the door and I rush to answer it when the familiar scent fills my nostrils.

I know who it is. I slowly open the door just enough to peer out.

"You're alive!" Erick gasped pushing the door open but I block it with my booted foot.

"How did you find me?" I scowled crossing my arms.

"It took a lot of work but we found you." He replied.

"We?"

"Ambrose is around." He replied looking over his shoulder.

"What do you want Erick?" I sighed.

"How did you cloak yourself? I mean—not even Ambrose could feel you. We were worried that you were . . . dead."

"Too bad huh," I attempted to shut the door when suddenly it whipped open and Ambrose is standing there leaning on the doorframe. I lost my balance for a quick second. "Go out." I pushed him away from the door. For the first time ever, I manage to knock him off balance, we both stood there shocked.

"Not until you tell me what is going on." Erick demanded.

"Why have you blocked me?" Ambrose asked steadying himself. "Better yet, how are you blocking me?"

I scoffed, "I want nothing to do with either of you." Just then, Lennox returned. I could hear his feet shuffle up the stairs as he approached. Both Erick and Ambrose turn around. I watched as Erick's face changed from shock to anger. I fought the urge to explain myself, as I always had in the past. I made it clear to the both of them that I was done with them. They do not need to know my business anymore.

"Is there a party I wisnae told abit?" He chuckled dropping his bag on the floor and shutting the door. I shook my head and leaned against the dresser.

"Evenin' lads." Lennox smiled, "Everythin' alright Sarah?"

"Wow, you seize to amaze me." Ambrose replied and turned towards me frowning, then looked back at Lennox. "Who the hell are you?" He asked.

"How's abit ye gezz yer name, then perhaps I'll gie ye mine." He replied. His accent made it hard to understand what he said. Erick didn't seem to be bothered by it. Lennox stalked towards Ambrose all puffed up. No one moved and no one offered any information. "Are these men botherin' ye Lass?"

"They were just leaving." I stated walking towards the door. Lennox pursed his lips and nodded while waiting for them to leave. I stood with my hand on the doorknob my eyes on the ground and my other hand on my hip.

"Ye heard the Lass, time tae go boys." He too walked towards the door. Erick did not say anything but I could feel his eyes on me. Ambrose eyed me up and down. My attire is what surprised him. I was wearing black leather pants with a matching jacket, a black leather bustier with dark red lace trim and knee high biker boots.

"You've changed." He said shaking his head.

"I wonder why." I snorted and crossed my arms.

"You know he's a witch right." Ambrose stated staring me in the eye and pointing at Lennox who stood directly behind me.

"And you're a filthy excuse for a human being. Oh wait sorry you're not human. I don't know what you are." I said and shoved him out door. We stared each other down. Lennox shut the door separating me and Ambrose.

My heart raced and I stood staring at the closed door until Lennox spoke.

"Friends ay yers?" He asked.

"Not anymore." I replied. He tossed the bag of cash at me with a big smile. I smiled back then dropped the bag on the table. I counted cash on the table piling them in bundles of a thousand each then wrapped an elastic band around them.

"Where did ye get this kin' ay cash," He asked stuffing the money back in the bag.

"That's none of your business." I replied.

Lennox thinned his lips and shrugged.

"We need to find a way to keep this safe and still have it available immediately. We can't take this much cash on a plane." I said.

"Agreed," He replied. "I ken someone."

"Is this person trustworthy?"

"Aye. I trust him with my ain life." He winked. I rolled my eyes at him. His charm was not going to win me over.

"Then let's do it. First things first," I pause a moment my index fingers gently stroking my bottom lip. "We need a car, something that won't be too noticeable and won't get broken into, while at the airport for however long we are away."

"Done," He dials a number then leaves the room. He shuts the bathroom door. I packed up my things then hauled the bag over my shoulder. As I walked out I ran right into Ambrose and Erick again.

"What now?" I crossed my arms and stepped back.

"You can't be left alone with a witch." Ambrose replied.

"I'm a witch. Besides, being with you two is no better, at least he hasn't tried to kill me." I stated, "I prefer to be alone but he just won't leave."

"I wonder why." Erick replied.

"Oh shut up Erick!" I snapped at him defensively. I know what Erick was thinking and he was wrong.

There was no attraction between Lennox and I. I backed up into the motel room again and slammed the door shut. Lennox came out of the bathroom to see what the commotion was. A grin formed across his lips when he spotted Erick and Ambrose had come back. "Who the hell do you think you are?" I yelled charging at them. Both Ambrose and Erick winced when I yelled. Lennox looked at them then at me. I stopped dead in my tracks, "What?"

"What the hell was 'at love?" Lennox asked.

"What was what?" I replied turning to face him.

"Dinnae play dumb wit' me, ye just caused them telepathic pain. I have never seen 'at before," He walked towards me.

"I—I don't know what you're talking about." I lied.

"Sure ye don't." He snorted. "I think I ken what they're sae afraid ay. If ye have abilities like 'at, I can only imagine what yer daughter is like." He replied.

"If this is going to be an issue you can leave." I replied. I leaned against the dresser again with my hands in my pockets.

"I told ye, I'm in this 'til the end." He replied. "I just spoke tae ma buddy, we can go an' see him in an hour." Lennox changed the subject.

"Good." I grabbed the bag. Ambrose and Erick just watched the two of us silently.

"What are we daein' wit' they two lads?" Lennox asked thumbing over his shoulder at the both of them.

"Nothing," I glower at them and walk out of the room. Ambrose stopped Lennox by grabbing his arm.

"What is your agenda Witch?" Ambrose hissed.

"I dinnae ken what yer talkin' abit." Lennox chuckled.

"You don't know what you are getting yourself into." He walked in front of him blocking his path.

"Och—I have a pretty good idea." He side stepped to get around him. Ambrose stared Lennox down. I could tell he was trying to get into his head. Lennox was very good at blocking his mind. Even I couldn't get in there.

"Sarah wait—" Erick said. I stopped and turned to look at him, "I want to help you." I glanced quickly at Erick then my eyes wandered until I could see Ambrose and Lennox by the car.

"Whatever," I said.

They had a car that was all that mattered right now. Erick and Ambrose sat in the front. I pulled Lennox away, even though I knew Ambrose would hear me, if he was paying attention.

"When the time comes, you kill that vampire." I said. Lennox looked over at Ambrose. "I can't do it."

"He is the one that Sired you isn't he?" He asked.

I did not answer. We had been talking for too long, Ambrose would be listening in by now. I climbed in behind Ambrose and Lennox walked around the back of the car to sit behind Erick.

"Where too," Ambrose asked.

"Used car lot," I replied.

"What for, I have a car." He scowled.

"No you have a beautiful piece of machinery that sticks out like a sore thumb everywhere we go. We need something more inconspicuous Ambrose."

"Fine," He said and pulled out of the parking spot.

The closest lot was only down the street. With the money spent in this town there was a car lot on every corner like it was a starbucks café. Ambrose arranged to trade his escalade in, for something more convenient, for our current situation. We all agreed on the car and the Sales man drew up the papers. After Ambrose signed the papers, the Sales man said the car would be ready tomorrow. A bit of a kink in the plans but we agreed.

Lennox gave Ambrose directions to where we were going to change the money. Without telling Ambrose, what we were doing, he got out and jogged a few blocks.

"So, how did you meet this Lennox character?" Ambrose asked. I knew that was coming. I could feel it festering inside him. I did not want to talk to him about that or anything for that matter. According to him, I was a vampire plague. I do nothing but make men fall in love with me then destroy them.

"Why do you care?" I asked. "He will die just like the rest." I snarled.

"I don't, just asking for Erick's sake," he replied.

"Don't involve me in your petty fights." Erick scoffed.

"You were involved the moment you entered my life again." I scowled then turned to face the window. I did not care anymore about what my words may have done to them. They hurt me more than I had ever been hurt before.

"I—" Erick attempted to speak but I cut him off.

"Stop talking!" I hissed. "I no longer want to hear anything from either of you, for this entire trip, unless it is an idea on how we are going to kill the council." I got out of the car. Both doors opened and the two of them hopped out.

"Kill the council? Sarah, are you crazy?" Ambrose shouted.

"Nope," I replied.

"You cannot take on the council!" Ambrose stated.

"I said don't talk, unless it is to discuss how to kill the council." I shouted and this time I saw what it did to them. I felt bad but I did not apologize for it. Lennox returned and broke the very thick tension in the air.

"I cannae leave ye alone fur a minute, without ye wantin' tae kill each other." He smirked touching my shoulder instantly calming me then he climbed in the back seat. He slid closer to me touching my leg. I pushed his hand off, looking up at him angrily.

"Don't." I crossed my legs and folded my hands in my lap.

"Everything alright?" he asked.

"For now," I replied.

"Where too," Ambrose asked. His knuckles white from gripping the stirring wheel.

"Food," I replied. Lennox nudged me. He handed me a card. Ambrose started the car and I leaned in towards Lennox.

"It's untraceable. Money is available twenty-four-seven." He said. I was not paying attention to where his hand was headed.

"All of it?" I asked feeling his fingers touch my hair.

"Minus what I paid to get his services," He replied with a slight shrug.

"How much is left?" I inched away. His hand touched my cheek brushing the hair from my face. I am sure that if Ambrose was watching right now, it must have looked like we were kissing.

"I took care of it." He replied with a casual 'it was nothing' shrug. I nodded and backed away. I could see Ambrose watching me in the mirror. Erick barely spoke two words since we got in the car again.

We pulled up to a dive bar and got out.

"What is this?" I asked placing my hands on my hips.

"You said you were hungry. No better place to get food for us and them, without anyone noticing." He said.

"I don't want—"

"I ken ay place, if ye dinnae want tae—" Lennox suggested gesturing a noose around his neck for his kill impression. I chuckled to myself turning away. Ambrose ignored the suggestion and walked in the direction of the bar. Erick glanced at me then turned and followed Ambrose. When we were alone, I decided to interrogate him.

"Are you really a witch?" I asked tucking my hands in my jacket pockets, walking in stride with Lennox.

"Aye."

"Did you always know?" I added.

"Aye."

"Have you always lived in Hartford?"

"Nah." He replied.

"What's with the one word answers?" I stopped walking.

"That's all they require." He laughed and turned to face me. I nodded then started walking again.

"You look a bit—blue."

"I'm just hungry." I replied quickening my pace.

"Nah, that's no' it." He turned, walked backwards and pointed his finger at me. "Somethin' abit the two Lads back there. What are they tae ye?"

"Doesn't matter," I brushed it off.

"Sure it does. They cam lookin' fur ye." He replied. "They care abit ye, an' I can tell ye care abit them."

"I'm sorry when did you become my therapist?" I scowled. He laughed, stopped then knocked on a random door, only it was not random, for him.

"I say what I see." He pointed to his eye then at me. I rolled my eyes and looked away.

"I wouldn't ask you to kill him if I cared, now would I?" He knocked again.

"I suppose your right." He replied. "Ye are a hard one to make out." The large peephole slid open and he whispered something to the person on the other side.

"Then quit trying." I replied. The door unlocked then opened. "We agreed there is no friendship here."

"Ladies first," He said gesturing for me to enter. "you agreed, no' me." He added. We walked down a long hallway and through a metal door. Lennox nodded and waved as we walked past people.

Inside the room at the end were wall-to-wall glass freezers. Top to bottom, filled with bags of frozen blood. In the center of the square room, chairs symmetrically placed, for human blood donors. All of which were currently in use. My mouth salivated, as the fresh coppery sweet smell filled my senses.

"They offer live donors, fresh pumped blood or frozen. Take yur pick, first ones on me." He chuckled. "Go ahead." He walked over to some guard at the door and started to talk to him. I watch as he exchanged money.

He then crossed his arms and stood like a soldier as I walked around eyeing the humans sitting in the chairs. A few of them glanced up and smiled. A girl sitting at a desk next to a tray full of tubes filled with blood, briefly glanced my way.

"What are those for?" I asked.

"Potential donors." She replied. I stared at her confused.

"Vampires have specific tastes." She smiled widely and her fangs showed. I nodded and continued to walk through the large room. I see a very cute blonde sitting in the back corner. He is sitting in his chair very relaxed. Our eyes locked and he sat up smiling.

"Him," I said to the girl at the desk. She walked over to him and looked over his file to see how much blood he had given already. Then she unhooked him from the machine. She placed a cold bottle of orange juice in front of him, which he downed in one gulp. He licked his lips and put the bottle on the desk. I slowly walked over to him. My fingers ran up his muscular arms.

"He'll do." I lean in taking in his scent. He smells very good. I noticed Lennox is watching me.

"This isn't a brothel honey. Fresh or bag, you choose." She said pointing to the chair where he was sitting.

"Is this your first time?" I asked the blond, turning my back to the abrupt Asian woman.

"Yes, I've actually never met—one of you before." He stuttered.

"I will be gentle, I promise." I smiled then take him in my arms. I caressed his face briefly then lean in close and bit down on his jugular. He gasped at first but as the blood filled me and my poison numbed him, I began to moan. His fingers grasped my jacket and I hear him gasp. I pulled away and he sits back doe eyed. "Not so bad huh," I whispered. He looked up at me forcing me to look away.

"You're so beautiful." He slurred.

"Miss, I think he is going to need another drink and maybe some food or something." I stuttered. She walked over with another bottle of juice, a sandwich and a multivitamins.

"He'll be fine. We have beds here. He'll sleep it off then go home and not even remember what went on here."

"Oh, so he has done this before?"

"Numerous times," She chuckled as if what I had just said was ridiculous. "He is one of our most highly recommended donors."

"How many times has his memory been erased?" I asked.

"I don't know, why do you care he's food," She scowled at me.

"That is inhumane you shouldn't be doing that to him." I could feel the temperature rise within me.

"That's calling the kettle black." She said, hands on her hips.

"I never erased his memory."

"No you didn't, but what did you expect would happen after you fed from him?" she asked.

"I don't know!" I shouted. She squinted and hovered over her desk. Lennox came running down the hall.

"You're a young vamp aren't you? You don't know the rules." She was about to charge at me.

"What's going on in here?" He grabbed my arm, looked at the Asian vampire and walked backwards, "Time tae go."

"No, he's coming with us." I replied.

"Are you crazy?" He snapped.

"No, do you realize what they do here?"

"Aye."

"How can you—"

He covered my mouth with his hand, "Sorry for the confusion. We'll be on our way." We make it to the door the whole time he is holding my mouth shut. So, I bit him.

"Ouch what'd ya do that fur?" He squeezed his hand.

"Go get him." I replied.

"No!"

"NOW!" I demanded

"Fine. Relax." He turned around, handed the guard and the girl some money and we take the guy with us. I tell her I want his name removed from their database. Whether or not she really did it I would never know.

"I hope you're happy, they'll never let us in there again."

"I don't care and how do you know about places like that?" I asked.

"I'm a witch Sarah, I hunt your kind. I make it a point tae ken where they hide oot." He stated. "Where tae hit them so it hurts."

"Duly noted."

"Not you, that's—the vampires—ach never mind." He shook his head and walked ahead of me. I laughed and took the nameless man by the arm leading him away from blood bank.

"Are we meetin' up with yur friends again?" He asked.

"They will just find me again if we don't." I sighed.

When we arrived back at the bar, I went inside to get Ambrose and Erick. I found them sitting in a booth, drinking. I stood at the head of the table, arms crossed. "Look at you two love birds." I joked.

"Funny." Erick replied.

"You done?"

"Yes." Erick replied.

"No," Ambrose chided.

"Let's go." I rolled my eyes at them. I turned to walk away when I felt someone grab me. I whipped around pulling free. Erick stared at me horrified.

"Can we talk?"

"I'm done talking." I said and walked away.

When we got outside Lennox was leaning against the wall having a smoke. He flicked it the moment our eyes met.

"That's a waste of a cigarette?" I said walking up to him. He shrugged.

"Tryin' tae quit anyway." He winked.

"Ready?" There was something about him that made me smile when he flirted.

"Aye," he answered.

"Is this a snack for later?" Ambrose asked.

"I'm sorry did you say something valid?" I snarled. The donor stood there helplessly confused. "Where do you live?" I asked the nameless man.

"I d-don't remember?" He replied.

"Great." Ambrose sighed.

We all loaded up in the truck. Erick sat in the front with Ambrose and I sat between Lennox and the donor. As we drove, I noticed the donor watching me. "What is your name?"

"Ken."

"Nice to meet you Ken, I'm Sarah. You are gonna stay with us for the night and hopefully tomorrow you will remember where you live." I explained.

"Thank you." He smiled dreamily. I frowned. Ambrose was watching us. He must be basking in his glory proving he was right once again. I did nothing to attract this man, he only remembered me saving him.

Well not really saving him because he never thought he was in danger . . . damn it. I laid my head back on the seat. It irritated me that Ambrose was right. I did all I could to keep him out of my head so that he didn't know what I was thinking. What was troublesome to me more than anything else was that vampires were capable of destroying someone and feeling no remorse over it. I tried to shake it off. Then I noticed that Ambrose was not watching me for once.

He was watching Lennox.

Chapter Seven

We pulled up to a hotel and each of us booked an individual room. Before I could say that Ken was staying with me, Lennox offered to take him. I thanked him and got in the elevator behind them. Ambrose took the penthouse as usual. The elevator doors opened on the tenth floor where Ken, Lennox and I got out. I made a left, the guys went right. I slid the card through the slot and the door unlocked. I flicked on the lights upon entering. Then I noticed that the door didn't click shut. When I turned around, Ambrose was standing there.

"I thought you were on the top floor." I snidely replied.

"I am, but I wanted to talk to you." He said shutting the door behind him.

"I doubt very much that I want to hear anything you have to say." I tossed my bag on the bed. I unzipped my jacket pulled it off and tossed it on the armchair.

"I need to talk to you, about what consists of our future plans."

"Go on." I unpacked a few things and placed them on the dresser provided.

"I think that going after the council with a witch, fallen angel and two vampires is suicide." He said.

"I will take that into consideration." I scoffed and turned away from him.

"Sarah I am not kidding." He grabbed my arm.

"I know you're not." I said pulling away.

"You have no idea what they are capable of." He replied.

I spun around angrily, "I am very clear on what they are capable of! I know what they did to Chase. I saw what they did to Jeff and his entire family. I know they will stop at nothing to kill me and Alaina after they get what they want." I screamed.

"What do they want?"

"Her blood what else," I answered.

"What for?"

"I don't know Ambrose, you have been a vampire for five hundred years what would they use her blood for?" I started to shout.

"You are on a downward spiral here Sarah. You need to step outside the box and really think about what you want to do here." He said following me around the room. "We need the facts and we need the numbers here Sarah. We cannot just rush in and take them out."

"Why not?" I know I was being unreasonable but I didn't care.

"They have so much power for one and for two; they probably know you are coming." He said.

"Good."

"They will kill you before you even leave the country." He grabbed me by the shoulders.

"How?" I asked freeing myself from his grasp. "I said how?"

"Plane crash," He said. "Assassin, who knows but they will not let you get to them first!"

"They would kill hundreds of innocent people just to stop me?"

"They don't care." He replied. My eyes widened at the thought of the plane going down and all those innocent lives taken from them because of me. "Do you see what I am talking about now? They don't care what they have to do to stop you." His hands cupped my face.

Tears welled in my eyes.

"We'll talk about this in the morning," I said holding his wrists and pulled his hands from my face. "I'm exhausted . . . please leave."

"You need to mend things with Erick."

"Tomorrow," I replied.

He did not move for a long time. He stared at me as though he had something more to say but never spoke another word. Then he broke the stare turned and walked towards the door. I locked the door once he was out and undressed quickly. Just after I pulled a long t-shirt over my head, there was a knock at the door. I peered through the hole to see Lennox standing there.

I opened the door a crack. "What's up?" I asked.

"I'm heedin' doon stairs fur a bit, is there anythin' ye need?" He asked leaning against the doorframe.

"I'm fine thanks, just going to sleep." I averted my eyes.

"Reit 'en, I'll see ye in the morn." He turned to walk way. "Oh by the way, Ken is oot fur the night."

"Okay." I replied biting my bottom lip. "Hey Lennox, can you help me with a few things?"

"Aye," He smiled turning back towards me.

"Not right now, tomorrow." I laughed. "I think I could learn a few things from you."

"How do ye mean?"

"You're a witch and well I'm a witch so I kind of have those abilities too." I screwed my lips.

"A witch-vampire, quite a deadly combination, how's it you're still alive?" He joked.

"Actually, I'm a hunter-witch-vampire." I corrected him. He glared at me then I see his jaw tighten. "What?"

"Naethin'," He backed away slowly, "I'll see you in the mornin'." I stepped out into the hall to watch him disappear around the corner. Then I went back in my room and locked the door again.

*****

Lennox made his way to the elevator glancing over his shoulder as he dialed a number on his cell phone. The voice on the other end answered. "I need tae speak with her right away." He demanded. There was silence for a few minutes then he said as the elevator doors sealed shut, "She's alive." He hung up and stuffed his phone in his jacket pocket. He got off on the ground floor and left the building.

*****

I grabbed a mini bottle of Rye from the bar fridge, unscrewed the cap and wrapped my lips around it. I sucked in air trying to relieve the burn in my throat. I was not much of a drinker but tonight I needed it. By the time the fridge was empty my eyes were heavy and I could feel myself drifting to sleep. I crawled into bed and buried myself in the blankets, when there was a loud knock at the door. "What now?" I whispered. I took a deep breath and slowly let it out. I grabbed the pillow covering my head. I tried to ignore the knocking but it did not stop. I rolled out of bed, walked across the room and opened the door only enough to show my face. "What!" I asked resting my head against the edge of the door. My eyes practically sealed shut. Erick appeared double so I closed one eye.

"Can I come in?" He asked.

"No." I tried to shut the door.

"Sarah."

"Erick." I mocked. "Where's your partner in crime?" I walked back to the bed.

"I don't know." He replied. I sat down on the bed with my legs crossed and leaned back on my hands until my body was too heavy for me to hold up and I fell back.

"What did you want to talk about?" I asked reminding him. He made his way across the floor and leaned against the dresser with his arms folded.

"Are you drunk?" He smirked.

"Yep," I waited patiently as he stood there staring at the ground. The annoyance grew. "So—"

He finally said. "I want you to understand, that the only reason I did what I did, was to protect you."

I sighed, bored of the same old story. "You told me that story already."

"It's not a story Sarah. I swear to you that I only wanted to make sure you didn't get yourself killed." Erick stepped towards the bed.

"Really Erick? People have been trying to kill me for over a year. Ambrose killed me once already this month and look at me, up and around feeling fine." I scoffed.

"You don't look fine, you look like someone who has let go of the fraying rope."

"Yeah well, maybe I have." I said closing my eyes. Erick walked closer and stood over me.

"I am sorry if I had any part in that. I never thought it would drive you to this." He stood over me.

"Drive me to what exactly?" I asked resting on my elbows.

"Suicide. This idea of yours is crazy."

"You remember the vision I shared with you right?" I asked standing up in an instant and our bodies practically touched.

"Do you remember it?" He mocked and stepped away. "We both die in that vision Sarah." He grabbed my shoulders.

"Yeah, well so do all of them." I replied. I took a step closer to him. His head jerked. "I told you not to come with us. You didn't listen."

"I couldn't." He replied. "However, I will this time. Because, I can't watch you die again. I can't be there to lose you all over again." He turned to leave.

"Well then, I guess it was good you already have." I followed him to the door.

"I said I was sorry! Why can't you believe me?" He stopped and turned towards me in one swift motion.

"So it's forgiveness you are looking for now?" I waited for him to answer but he never did. "I'm all out of forgiveness, Erick." I walked past him towards the door and he grabbed my hand reeling me to him. "Don't you dare!" I pushed him away. He tried again but this time I pinned him against the wall. Teeth barred. My anger inside was getting the best of me. "Do you want to die?"

"Yes . . ." tears spilled from his eyes. "If it means that I will stop feeling this way, then yes, kill me." My heart panged and I dropped my hands at my sides. My eyes watered and it felt as if I was about to hyperventilate.

"No, don't do this to me again." I cried pointing my finger at him and backing away.

"I am not doing anything!" He shouted.

"You are making those feelings come back and I don't want them too!" I shouted wiping my face.

"You will hate yourself if you push those feelings away. You will become like him . . . Like Ambrose."

"Ambrose!" I gasped, grabbed the key-card and stormed out the door.

"Where are you going?" He chased after me. I did not bother with the elevator. I dashed up the stairs to the floor just below the penthouse then took the elevator. "Sarah! Why are you going to him? You're not even dressed."

"I don't require clothes to kill him."

"When it comes to him you do, you know he wants you and showing up in a t-shirt an inch short of your—"

"Stop!" I turn and shove my hand in his face. "You no longer have a say in what I do! You lost that privilege when you destroyed any humanity left in me!" My hands made contact with his chest and I shoved him. Erick grabbed the wall to stop himself from falling. His eyes widened. I could feel the rage inside burning and screaming to get out. I looked down at my hands. My eyes widened. I turned away from him and knocked loudly on the door nonstop until he answered.

"What?" He groaned looking me up and down, "Come in." He smirked.

"I figured you would be out," I snarled.

"Yeah well, I wasn't in the mood. However, you may change that." He smiled until Erick came around the corner. "Or not," He rolled his eyes.

I got right to the point of my visit, "Tell me about when you changed." I stopped directly in front of him with my arms across my chest.

"Why, what does that matter?" He asked.

"Just tell me!" I screamed like a child having a tantrum.

"I'd do as she says." Erick gestured crazy with his finger at his temple.

"You can leave now Erick." I said without turning to face him.

Ambrose's left brow rose and his lip curved slightly. He walked around the room and I could feel the uneasiness coming from both of them.

"Zadkiel attacked me one night, said he wanted to kill me but something about me made him change his mind." He poured three glasses of amber liquid into three crystal glasses then handed us each one.

"What did he see?" I asked gulping the brandy down then held my breath as it burned.

"Potential," he replied.

"What about your wife?"

"He killed her." He said and looked out the window.

"Why?"

"Why does Zadkiel do anything?" He snapped looking over his shoulder at me. "For his own personal pleasure," he turned away. "Why do you want to know this anyway?" his voice almost inaudible.

"Because I do," I said and turned to leave.

"What relevance does this have with our current situation?" He asked pouring the brandy in our glasses again.

"It doesn't, nothing you say or do is relevant. It's just that for the first time since you changed me, I feel nothing." I had to hold back the tears. "All I feel is anger, hate and rage. All I can think about is killing, and blood and sex."

"Welcome to vampire-ville." He chuckled. Erick glanced at him then me. "I wouldn't worry about it, you couldn't hurt a fly." He laughed.

"I killed you didn't I."

"Killed—being past tense." He laughed, "You tried to kill me Sarah and clearly you didn't succeed."

"I'll try harder next time." I scowled and made my way to the door.

"Is this a game?" Erick asked pure annoyance in his voice. "Is all a big joke to the both of you?"

"You want it to be angel boy?" Ambrose craned his neck to look over at Erick with a big smile.

"A child's life is at stake here people and you two seem to enjoy pissing each other off instead of looking for her!" Erick shouted.

"Excuse me!" I retorted.

He looked over at Ambrose ignoring me completely, "Look, I think you are right about going in guns blazing. It's crazy and wreckless. I say we gather up our numbers, find anyone who is crazy enough to join us and then go."

"What about Draven?" Ambrose asked.

"All I can do is ask," I said then walked out of the room. Surprisingly, Erick did not follow me. When I got back to my room, the door was open. I slowly approached, peering in. The room was too dark, to tell if someone was in there. Then it opened all the way and Lennox was standing there.

"There you are Lass, out for a wee stroll I see." He laughed shutting the door behind me. "Where are yer clothes?"

"Who's this?" I asked crossing my arms.

"This is someone who wants tae speak wit' ye." He said clearing his throat.

"Why?"

"You are right Lennox, she is abrasive." She laughed.

"I believe she is that way because of all the shite that has happened tae her." he replied.

"Enough of the history lesson, explain to me what is going on and who this is." I stood between them.

"I'll tell you who I am dear. Have a seat." She watched me closely as I made my way to the armchair by the window. I crossed my legs and arms and just stared. Lennox sat back on the table with one leg up off the ground. I watched him as he lit a smoke and let out a billowing breath.

"So, who are you?" I asked impatiently.

"I'm your mother." She blurted.

At first, I thought I imagined what she just said to me. But, the look on her face did not falter. She was dead serious.

"Excuse me?" I laughed.

"I'm your mother." She repeated.

"How?"

"I would assume you don't need a lesson on baby making." She chortled. Laughter irritated me easily these days. I jumped to my feet but Lennox jumped in my way.

"Just cam doon Lass," He placed a hand on my shoulder. I was as surprised as the woman was on how Lennox could stop me. I glared at him and he let me go.

"It's okay Len." She touched his shoulder. He turned his head slightly and then stepped back.

"I was told you were both dead. Wait—are you my father?" I glanced at Lennox. He laughed and choked on the smoke. He shook his head laughing and coughing.

"Och thanks a lot." He laughed. "We're the same age."

"Well you look pretty young yourself." I motioned towards Moira.

"Good jeans." Moira grinned.

"What's this about, why are you showing up now?"

"I have been looking for you for twenty years." She replied.

"What? I don't understand. I thought you sent me away to protect me, or so I was told."

"No, your father's grandmother sent you away." She replied.

"I don't understand."

"Long story short, no one ever accepted our marriage. It was wrong for a hunter to marry a witch." She looked up at Lennox then back at me. "Nothing your father and I said would stop them."

"Why didn't she just kill me, why send me away and protect me?"

"It is not in our blood to kill a child, regardless of their bloodline. And I was the one who put the protection spell on you."

"That would explain the past two years."

"What do you mean?" She asked sitting on the arm of the chair.

"Strange things started to happen around me which now explains a lot about my abilities."

"Hence my reaction tae yer telepathic powers," Lennox added.

"So I'm quite the mixture of species huh. A witch, hunter, vampire, what else don't I know." I sighed.

"Your father's family blood line goes back a long way. Some of them were Nephilim. Most hunters are."

"That would explain the markings then." I said to myself.

"Markings?" She asked. I turned around pulled the shirt over my head. Lennox turned away. My 'mother', flicked the switch on the light by the bed then walked over to me.

"The markings fade once it's been scorched into my skin."

"This is incredible." I could feel her fingers brush along the marks.

"Not really." I frowned and pulled my shirt down.

"You are the most powerful being on this earth darling. No one can hurt you."

"Oh they can and they have." I said. I sat back down, crossed my legs and tapped my fingers on the arm of the chair. "So what now?"

"I am going to join you. You could use my help." She said.

"Let's say, that everything you told me is true. Did you think that I would just say, yeah sure, come along. Join us in our death match, why not, the more the merrier." I replied loudly. She laughed then leaned forward.

"You trust Lennox?"

"Not entirely." I glanced up at him. He smiled and looked away. I stared at her for a long time. They both waited anxiously for me to say something. "I don't want your help." I got up and walked over to the bed. "I'm sure you can see your way out." I pulled the blankets off and climbed in.

"Sarah." She said, "Please let me help you. If there is anything that I owe you, it is my protection. You don't know how much it hurt me, to lose you."

"I am sure I do." I replied. "Where is my father?" I added.

"He died a long time ago." She replied.

I took a deep breath then said. "We plan on gathering as many people as possible. Once we have the numbers, we leave for Europe."

"I know of some people that would help." She replied.

"Good. Bring whomever you want. I don't care as long as I get to destroy the council that is all that matters to me right now."

"You have taken on a dark path here Sarah. With your powers, that could be very dangerous," she stated.

"Good night." I scowled and turned over. I closed my eyes and listen for the click of the door shutting. I did not fall asleep instantly, instead my mind raced with everything I had just learned.

My mother was alive? How true was this? Can Lennox be trusted? These were all valid questions and no one to banter with to figure it all out. I started to long for the comfort Chase use to give me, when he was alive. He was someone I could always go to. Someone I trusted.

Chapter Eight

Lennox

"What'ur we gonnae dae Moira?" Lennox asked rubbing his chin then crossed his arms.

"I really don't know. She's a ticking time bomb. What happened to her?" She asked.

"They two lads taggin' along, they are the ones causin' her grief." He explained.

"Bring me to them." She replied.

Together they took the elevator to the penthouse suite. Lennox figured they should meet the vampire first. To their surprise, they found them together. Ambrose glared at the woman in front of him. She looked and smelled oddly familiar.

"Do I know you?" He asked letting them in. Erick was standing by the window, his arms folded. He glanced over his shoulder.

"I wanted to introduce you to someone." Lennox replied taking his hand out of his pockets and placing them on Moira's shoulders. "She would like to help out."

"Why is that?" Ambrose was suspicious.

"She is Sarah's mother." Erick whispered. Moira's eyes slowly glanced over at Erick. She watched as he moved towards her.

"You're the Angel." She nodded approvingly.

"Was," He corrected.

"Pity," She shrugged. "I think Sarah is in serious danger, from herself. She has a lot of anger building inside and I think that if we don't stop her, she will explode and that will be catastrophic for us all."

"We are well aware." Ambrose replied annoyed.

"Then why haven't you done anything about it." She asked.

"All she cares about now is finding her daughter. Once she has her daughter back, everything will be fine."

"You really believe that?" She asked. They both nodded. "Then you are both dumber than I thought. They will not have her daughter. If anything, her daughter is already dead. Going there and fighting them won't bring her back."

"What makes you think she is dead?" Erick asked.

"The council doesn't keep their prisoners alive for very long." She said. "You are an Angel you should know this."

"How do you know this?" Ambrose asked.

"I just know." She glowered at the both of them.

"If we try to stop her, she will go without out us." Erick replied.

"I haf'tae agree wit' ye there." Lennox replied. "I've only ken the Lass a short while but I can see she is determined."

"Fine, we stick to the plan. We must protect her at all costs." She waited for them all to agree then she headed towards the door. "Why did you turn her?" Moira asked before she left.

"She died." Ambrose replied and looked away. Moira looked at Erick then back at Ambrose.

"You love her too huh." He never answered. She scoffed and walked out.

*****

The next morning I was still in bed when someone knocked on the door. I groaned as I pulled off the warm blankets and ran across the cold room to the door. When I opened it, Erick was standing there.

"Everything alright?" I asked groggily.

"I don't know." He replied handing me a lunch bag.

"What's this?" I yawned.

"Food." He replied and sat down on the bed. I opened the bag to find a few pints of blood.

"They are warm?" I asked surprised.

"I asked them to warm them for you." He said.

"Thanks." I opened the first one and drank it fast. "Where are the others?"

"In bed I guess." He replied.

"What time is it?" I asked and lied across the bed to see the alarm clock. "It's six in the morning Erick. Why are not you sleeping?" I pouted turning over. I stared at the ceiling.

"I can't sleep." He replied. I sat up and stared at him a moment, before getting off the bed open the other bag of blood.

Then I searched my bag for my toothbrush. "Well crash there then. I'm done sleeping anyway." I said and shut the bathroom door. When I came out, Erick was still sitting on the edge of the bed. "When are you leaving?"

"I'm not," He whispered, "I met your mother." He added fiddling with something in his hand.

"So she claims."

"She is your mother Sarah, it so obvious."

"How is it obvious Erick? Have you met my mother before?" I replied.

"No, not personally but I have seen her before. When you were a baby," He replied looking up at me.

I waived my hands trying to distract him, "Your changing the subject, why aren't you leaving now?"

"I changed my mind." He said matter-of-factly.

"Erick!" I said stuffing the paste and brush in my bag. "You die in my vision, remember."

"Yeah well, that was the plan from the beginning right." He replied. "I die protecting you, man upstairs says so."

"Yeah when you were on his side and he wasn't pissed at you for loving me." I knelt down in front of him. "Don't do this please. I have lost enough already, don't be someone else I will have to miss."

"What does it matter anymore? You won't forgive me. You practically shunned me from your life." He said then gently pushed away so he could stand up, "It would hurt me more to be away from you, than if I die."

"Stop it." I stood up. "Don't do this to me. Not now Erick!"

"I'm sorry Sarah." He walked towards the door. My stomach started to do flips and I felt like I was going to be sick. "Like I said I changed my mind." His hand touched the handle and I ran at him.

"No!" I grabbed him. "I love you. I'm not going to let you die for me!" He pried my hands off his arms.

"You are only saying that to stop me."

"No I'm not." I retorted. "You know that I love you. I may be angry with you but my feelings have never changed."

"You can't forgive me. How could I possible believe you still love me?" He said shaking his head. "I am not that stupid Sarah."

"Stop." I shouted.

"I'm going back to my room." He opened the door and walked out.

What a start to my morning. I screamed at him throwing my hands up in the air. Why did Erick have to bait me like this? I know why he was doing it. He wanted me to say I forgave him. I did not want to give him the satisfaction of forgiving him because I was still hurt. Another knock at the door, I opened it quickly hoping to find Erick there but it was Lennox.

"Don't you sleep?" I scoffed.

"Aye," He laughed. "Early mornin'?"

"Apparently," I sighed walking towards the chair and flopped down on it.

"What's bothering ye the-day?"

"What isn't bothering me," I rolled my eyes.

"Come on now, it cannae be that bad."

"It's Erick."

"Wha' abit him?"

"It's a long story."

"I have all day." He smiled. I smiled back.

"He wants me to forgive him but I am having trouble doing that. But if I don't, he will come with us which isn't a good idea because he has lost his powers." I said.

"Why has he lost his powers? I thought he was an Angel or somethin'?"

"Yeah well, he was until he fell in love with me and couldn't stay away and blah, blah, blah. He was warned and didn't listen so now he's human." I said.

"That's bollocks." He replied. "So now he wulnae leave coz ye cannae forgive him."

"Right."

"Then just dae it. Who cares if ye mean it! If it keeps him alive Hen, what does it matter if ye dae or dinnae? Just forgive the Lad coz in the end what's said an' done, wulnae matter if yer both deed."

"Thanks." I replied.

"Anytime," He smiled.

"I'll see you later?"

"Where ye going?"

"To forgive," I replied. I heard him chuckle then the door clicked shut. I got dressed then made my way to Erick's room. I knocked on the door but he did not answer. I spot the maid, down the hall and ran over to her. "Excuse me miss, I forgot my key inside can you let me in?" I asked. She eyed me a moment then followed me down the hall. I thanked her and slipped into the darkness and made my way across the room. My eyes focused and I could see Erick's body in the speck of light that crept through the blinds. He was lying on his chest, with the blankets just at his waist and his arms hugging the pillow. I knelt down on the floor next to the bed.

"Erick." I whispered. His body jerked slightly then he turned towards me. His one eye opened.

"Hey." He groaned.

"Shush. I didn't want to wake you but I just wanted to tell you something. Don't get out of bed." I started. He laid his head back down on the pillow his hand on the edge of the bed. I couldn't resist I had to touch his face and ran my fingers through his curly brown hair.

"What's the matter?" He asked. I watched his eyes slowly blink, as he fought to stay awake.

"I forgive you." I finally said. His entire face tensed and he clenched his teeth. I could see the goose bumps form on his skin. I reached up and gently touched his face again. His eyes shut and I can feel that his breathing had sped up. My other hand slides in between the pillow and his jaw and I caressed his cheek. "I love you." Before he could say anything, I leaned in close and kissed him. He extended the arm closest to me and slinked his fingers in my hair. I tried to stand up but he moved with me and pulled me to him. I held my breath and tried not to fight. He had to believe what I was saying.

"I just wanted to tell you that." I said and backed away from him.

"So—that I would leave," He asked. He sat up, legs off the side of the bed.

"No, so that you would know," I tried to sound convincing. He got out of bed and that was when I noticed he was very naked. I glanced away. He slowly walked towards me.

"What made you change your mind?" He asked.

"Do you always sleep in the nude?" I laughed nervously closing my eyes. I slowly backed away towards the door.

"I wasn't expecting anyone." He stopped next to me his arm slung around my waist. I gripped the doorknob but when I tried to open it, Erick's long strong arm stretched out over my head holding it shut. I looked up and he was looking down at me. My heart raced.

"I love you." He whispered. I bit my lip and completely lost myself in his stare. I feel his hand move up my back as he leaned down to kiss me. I wrapped my arms around his back. His thumb bushed across my cheekbone as he pulled back to look at me. My eyes watered.

"I should go." I gasped, trying so hard not to break down. The light from the bathroom seeped through the slightly ajar door. He licked his lips and they glistened like the twinkle of freshly fallen snow under the bright morning sun. He did not move but he did lean in to kiss me again, slowly and gently. My heart began to melt. I gave in and let my emotions take hold. I can feel his fingers playing with the hem of my shirt. I raised my arms allowing him the ability to take off my shirt. It dropped to the floor. His warm strong hands gently stroke my shoulders. He brushed my hair away and gently stroked my skin. My eyes closed and I inhale his scent. His fingers fiddled with my bra a moment and then it fell to the floor. He unbuttoned my pants pulling them down enough until they fall to the ground on their own. His hand laced mine as he led me to the bed. My entire body swarmed in goose bumps. All I want is for him to touch me. It's all I can think about.

That was when he stepped away. He stood there and stared at me. His eyes glossy, his lips inches from mine. His breathing, laboured and I can tell he was trying to pace himself. This time, I touched him first. I ran my hand flatly against his skin up his chest then down his arms. I leaned in and kissed his shoulder, slowly moving closer to his neck. His arms wrapped around my waist and he turned his head so our lips touched.

His mouth slightly parted and his tongue moved in to touch mine. His thumbs hooked the inside elastic of my lace panties, he sat on the edge of the bed and pulled them down. He ran his fingers up my inner thigh and I couldn't help my legs from wobbling. His kiss caresses my navel and his hands grip my buttocks. I twisted my fingers in his curly hair. My head flung back as his tongue ran up my stomach and he pulled my nipple into his mouth. I groaned. Then ever so smoothly yet quickly, his mouth is on mine again and our tongues violently dance. He playfully bites down on my bottom lip just as I dig my nails into his back. He sucked in air at the twinge of painful pleasure it caused him. I pressed hard against his mouth and he lifted me up, turned around and laid me on the bed. The burning between my legs was gently but firmly satisfied moments later and I gave myself to him.

Erick's fingers tracing along my naked flesh, as I lay next to him. My bare shoulder welcomed his kiss. My body thrived for the firm grip his hands offered my breasts. He leaned in close to tell me he loved me. I turned toward him and smiled telling him I loved him too.

For that one hour we were together I had forgotten who I was. I forgot that I was a monster who needed to drink human blood to survive. Someone who cannot love without consequences and as I think about all this, tears began to fill my eyes and I cannot control the tears.

"What's wrong?" He asked twirling his fingers in my hair.

"Promise me you will go home and wait for me there." I pleaded.

"Sarah—"

I interject his plea, "No, I love you and I don't want to lose you please for once, just listen to me." I leaned on my arm and reach out to touch his cheek with my hand. Unfortunately, there was a knock at the door and then it opened. Well it was more like, the door opened then the knock came. And of course, it was Ambrose. Who else could I have expected it to be?

"Sorry I didn't realize you weren't alone."

"I'm sorry I didn't know you had a key?" I scowled.

"I thought you weren't speaking." He looked around the room where my clothes had been scattered.

"Done and over with," I sat up and pulled the sheet over me.

"I figured we would all meet in my room to discuss what's next." He replied.

"Okay." Erick replied.

"In an hour," I smirk.

"An hour?" Erick turned to look at me. I smiled then he smiled. "Yeah an hour sounds good." He nodded and glanced back over at Ambrose.

"Whatever." Ambrose rolled his eyes then left.

"I love pissing him off." I laughed.

"Don't use me to do that." He attempted to get out of bed but I grabbed him and pulled him back.

"I said an hour."

"Yeah, I figured to get changed and eat?"

"Okay then hour and a half." I laughed and climb on top of him. This time we rushed so that we can meet up with everyone but we also had a shower together and made love in there too. He allowed me to drink from him. I really underestimated how much I did love him. I could not help but giggle and eye him, as we dressed. He did the same and it felt as though I was in high school all over again. We held hands as we left the room and got on the elevator. He kept glancing over at me, and I him. Then I grabbed him and kissed him. The elevator doors opened and someone got in, we leaned against the wall of the elevator and tried to act innocently.

The doors opened at the penthouse suite and we get out. Flash backs of the day I found Ambrose and his guards murdered on the penthouse floor flooded my mind. I gasped and stopped walking. Erick stopped with me.

"Are you alright?" He asked.

"I—I think something is wrong?" I clenched at my chest.

"What?"

"I don't know." I replied.

I pushed through the door and find that they are all sitting there waiting for us. I gulped and sat down glaring at Ambrose. He was projecting those images in my mind. I scowled and he just gave me an evil smirk.

"We have been able to reach out to some friends who are willing to help." Moira started.

"That's—great." I replied.

"Well—we have also alerted a few covens that we are gearing up to take on the council."

"Nonetheless, we leave in a week." I said.

"Good." Moira stood up.

"Lennox and I have some things to take care of. We'll be back in a few hours." I stated.

"Where are you going?" They all asked surprised. I shook my head laughing.

"None of your business," I replied and headed for the door, "Coming Lennox?"

"Aye," He replied and followed me.

Chapter Nine

"So where we going Lass?" Lennox asked once we were outside.

"To the nearest forest."

"You plan on whacking me?" He laughed.

I laughed, "No, I plan on learning from you." I shook my head at him.

"Och I see, the power thing."

"Yeah, I believe you can help me in this area."

"Aye, I can." He stuffed his hands in his pockets and we walked briskly in the opposite direction of the hotel. I was not sure if this was a good thing or not. I did not know the magnitude of my powers yet.

"This should be good." I said stopping in the middle of a field.

"Maybe we should find a place closer to water just in case." He chuckled.

"Sure." We walked farther in until we found a tiny stream. "This is good." I let out an uneasy breath.

"Alright, what dae ye want tae learn first?" He asked.

"Honestly I don't know. I know I can use fire and most recently telekinesis. Maybe use both together." I replied.

"'at is far tay advanced fur ye."

"There's no time to learn everything. Clearly, vampires are afraid of fire so—let's concentrate on that, and if I can control them while on fire then that works for me." I said.

"Sounds good," He screwed his lips.

We started with building a ball of fire in my palm. I do not know how long we were going at it but by the time I looked up, the sun started to set. I was able to manage and control the fire, manipulating it to do what I wanted it to do by the time the sun was completely out of the sky. Lennox on the other hand was starting to feel the power of my telekinesis, so we had to stop until he could cast a protective spell against it. I managed to control how I projected it too, which will come in handy.

"Thanks a lot. I really appreciate you showing me a few things." I said.

"Ye dinnae need tae thank me." He replied with a smile. Then something strange happened. He looked at me in a way I never expected. He was so close to me that I started to feel uncomfortable.

"We should head back." I said pulling away. I followed behind him as we began to walk back to the hotel. He kept glancing back at me and I just smiled at him. I never noticed it before. Well I certainly did not expect it. We were almost out of the forest when something grabbed me. I could not move or speak, whatever it was had complete control over me. All I could do was pray Lennox would turn around, soon.

"Sarah?" He said, finally turning. "SARAH!" He shouted and ran to me but whatever it was lifted his hand and suspended Lennox in the air. "Let . . . her . . . go!" He said clawing at his throat as if trying to pry fingers from it.

"Haec mea est!" He said. *'She is mine.'*

"Let her go." Lennox repeated.

"Numquam!" He growled. *'Never!'*

"You'll *'exsisto sollicitus."* Lennox replied. *'You'll be sorry.'*

Before the creature could do anything else, Lennox began chanting something and seconds later, the creature dropped me. I fell to my knees then crawled away. I could see the ball of fire in Lennox's hand grow bigger and bigger. I stood up, balled my hands and willed the fire to my palms. Together we blasted the creature. After a few clean hits, it vanished.

"What the hell was that?" I asked breathlessly as we turned and ran.

"A Demon," He replied.

"How did it find us?" I asked. My feet hit the pavement and we slowed down.

"They can sense our powers when we use them. It's the easiest way they can track us. Not a good thing for us." He said.

"Clearly," I sighed and opened the door to the hotel lobby. "What does he want from us?"

"Same thing everyone wants from witches—power."

"Again with the power," I rolled my eyes. "I don't even know how to use it. Well not properly."

"It disnae matter. They can still wield yer powers e'en if ye dinnae realize ye have it." He replied.

"Great."

"You're the key. A witches power is the ultimate power but a witch as powerful as ye, could give them the control they need to take over the world. Which is every demons dream come true." He explained.

"This just keeps getting better and better." I said rolling my eyes.

"I wudnae worry abit it. Ye have some powerful frien's around tae protect ye. Ye dinnae have tae dae this alone."

"That is where you are wrong." I said feeling my body tremble.

"What dae ye mean?" He asked.

"I mean I don't want anyone else to die just to protect me. I have already lost so much. So many families are suffering because of me." The elevator door opened.

"You cannae blame yourself Lass. They chose to be with ye. You're no' forcin' anyone to dae it." He said and grabbed my arm.

"How do you know that?" I opened the door to the penthouse suite. Everyone turned to look at us. "It's because of me that they offer to do it. If they didn't know of me, everyone would be safe." I wiped my face.

"Dinnae be foolin yourself Lass. They all choose to be here, includin' me and yer mother."

"Right . . ." I sighed.

"What's 'at supposed tae mean?" He asked insulted.

"Everyone always has an ulterior motive." I replied.

"Well I dinnae, an' I'm nae claimin' tae be innocent. I was lookin' fur ye, as per yer mother's request. Nae hidden agenda here!" He said sternly. "Besides, if I wanted ye dead, you'd be dead." He stressed out the last part.

"That's what everyone says." I replied.

"What are you talking about?" Erick asked walking towards me.

"We were just attacked outside." I replied. The bruises on my neck were just starting to disappear.

"What!" Moira asked.

"Demon," I replied eyeing Moira.

"A demon that's strange." She said.

"Not really. Strange things happens more commonly around me, than you may think." I replied.

"I meant as in, how easily they found you."

"Well it is pretty convenient that a demon showed up to attack me when you come to town." I snapped.

"Also, not what I meant," She looked over at Lennox queerly. "A demon attacks when they sense power." She corrected me.

"She is right Sarah." Erick replied. I didn't say anything else. If Erick agreed with her then she must be telling the truth, and if anyone knew about demons, it was Erick.

"If I learned to shield myself from them, would I be safe?" I asked.

"Perhaps. But there isnae a guarantee," Lennox replied.

"No harm in trying. I can't have anything standing in my way right now." I replied.

"I will teach ye everythin' ye want tae know." Lennox said. "We need tae go somewhere far. Somewhere close to nature. It is easy to protect when there are less manmade elements around."

"I know just the place." Erick replied.

"No I told you that you have to leave." I stated.

"This is the path that I have chosen Sarah. I am ready to die, and you will just have to accept that?" He said matter-of-factly.

"Maybe I will lock you up like you did me." I said.

"I'd like to see you try." He laughed and walked away from me.

"Don't tempt me." I said then turned to leave. Lennox and Erick attempted to follow me but I stopped them. "Alone." I said, raised my hand and stopped them.

"She is getting stronger by the minute." Erick replied feeling the power emanate from me.

"Ye have no idea the amount ay power she holds." He said turning back towards the room. Erick watched Lennox disappear down the hall.

Then he followed me. He didn't think I knew he was there but I did. I found a variety store and asked the clerk if they sold rope. She walked me to the isle. I grabbed two and brought them back to the check out. I paid the clerk then walked out and walked right into Erick. I laughed then walked around him.

"I'm sorry." He replied embarrassed.

"Your stealth abilities are terrible." I laughed.

"I know." He blushed. "It's not the same when you can smell me coming." We both laughed and I slinked my fingers with his. He squeezed my hand and this time I did not let go. It was the strangest feeling holding his hand this way. It felt almost—normal. "What did you buy?"

"Rope."

"For what?"

"You," I smirked.

"Kinky."

"I'm dead serious." I stopped and stared him down. "You are not coming."

"You can't tie me up." He replied ripping his hand from mine.

"Watch me."

"I know some people in England that will join us." He added.

"Fine," I replied. What could I say? We needed all the help we could get.

Back at the hotel Ambrose had left to feed and Lennox and Moira were nowhere to be found.

"I think we should contact Draven to see if he will help." I grabbed the phone and dialled his number. Draven picked up after a few rings. The conversation with Draven was brief but he agreed to help as best he could. The safest way we could meet with him was off the island.

Chapter Ten

The next morning we all met in the lobby. Draven and Victoria were waiting for us. None of us attempted to greet the other. We all took separate cabs and met at another location in the outskirts of town. One by one we arrived and started through the deserted area before the next cab arrived with the following person. I watched everyone arrive. Lennox and Moira kept to themselves, as did Ambrose. Erick stayed close to me. Draven and Victoria arrived last but together.

"So what is the plan?" Draven asked once we were finally alone.

"The plan is to take a flight out to Europe and gather as many people as we can, starting in England. The stronger we are the better off we are. And I can have my daughter back." I replied.

"I know some people as well. I will make some calls. Victoria and I have already packed up and left. We are staying close by." He said.

"Good. If you suspect anything, leave. We can't lose the upper hand here." I added.

"What makes you think we have the upper hand?" Ambrose chided.

"Always the optimist right Ambrose." I scowled. He rolled his eyes and looked away. "Anyway—keep in close contact. If you hear anything or something happens, tell one of us. Everyone exchange numbers before we leave."

"Why?"

"Well, if I'm hurt and I need help, I may try to call for help. If I only have—say your number, I'm screwed if you're already dead." I replied. Moira and Lennox nodded approvingly. "Good and I am not going back to that hotel. It was too close to the most recent attack."

"You were attacked?" Victoria asked.

"Yes." I looked straight at her, "Demon." She looked over at Draven.

"We will meet up at the airport in five days. Make sure your contacts know when we are arriving. I will order our tickets, apart from us everyone will have to find their own way there. If they don't arrive when we do, then we leave without them. I can't wait any longer. Is that clear?"

"Sir yes sir." Ambrose snarled and saluted.

"You don't have to come you know. You and your sarcasm can stay here," I replied.

"What's with him?" Draven asked watching Ambrose stomp away.

"Lover's quarrel," Lennox laughed. "Lennox's the name," He introduced himself and offered his hand. Draven smiled and accepted then introduced Victoria.

"Pleasure," Lennox bowed and kissed her hand. "See you soon." He said and left with Moira.

"Who are they?" Draven asked.

"I don't know about him but, she claims to be my birth mother."

"You're kidding?" Victoria gasped.

"No, I don't have enough information to say she isn't. So, I just gotta play it out, see what happens. She's a witch my father was a hunter—Angel thing. I'm a mutt." We all smiled. "It's all so friggen complicated." I said with a sigh.

"I can see that." Draven tried to smile.

"See you soon Sarah, take care of yourself." Victoria added and they left.

"Oh Sarah, before I forget, this was left for you." He said handing me an envelope.

"Who's it from?" I asked looking at the writing.

"Chase." He replied.

My brow furrowed and I had to swallow the vomit that rose in my throat. Erick stood next to me not saying a word. I tucked the letter in my back pocket and walked back to the main road.

I could not stop thinking about the letter. I wanted to read it but I also wanted to rip it up and throw it away. I left Erick so I could feed. It was still daylight for another three hours. We walked a few miles before we found a motel. I made my way to our room while he settled the bill. When he arrived he opened the door for me. I went straight to the bathroom and sat down on the toilet holding the white envelope in my shaking hand.

'Find me.'

I wiped the tears from my eyes and stuffed the paper back in the envelope. All that paper for two words.

Find me? What did that even mean?

My heart, felt as though it was ripped from my chest. When I walked out of the bathroom, Erick was sitting on the edge of the bed.

"What's wrong?" He asked. I didn't say a word. Instead, I handed him the note and left the motel room to go for a walk.

When I returned, Erick greeted me with a hug. "I'm sorry."

"You don't have to be." I sighed. "I think I am use to this by now, or maybe I should be—I don't know." I mumbled and waved my hands in frustration.

"I just wish I could make it all go away. Make you happy again." He said kissing my cheek. "Before all of this, you smiled all the time."

"I hope I will feel that way again soon." I said turning around. "I just wish I knew what that was supposed to mean? Is he alive?" I touched Erick's perfectly sculpted face, and stared into his awesome green eyes. "You know what—it doesn't matter. I won't let anyone play with my mind anymore. For all I know Ambrose wrote that note." I said sitting on the bed. "I think when all is said and done, I need a long secluded vacation."

"I agree." He smiled and brushed the hair way from my face. "I think if Chase were alive someone would know."

Our lips gently touched. I tucked my hair behind my ears and back away. "I can't wait to actually begin my life—well what's left of it." He didn't say anything just continued to stare at me. "We can finally have everything we ever wanted."

"Yes we can." He said taking my hand in his.

Chapter Elven

I tossed and turned all night while Erick seemed to have had the best sleep of his life. Every time I closed my eyes, I would see death, images of the end of the world, of someone finally killing me or my child.

Now it was dawn.

Erick never said anything to me when he woke up. He offered to drive though. I was too exhausted to argue. He kept his eyes on the road but held my hand in his, the entire drive.

"Thank you." I whispered then let my eyes close on their own.

"For what?" He asked glancing over quickly.

"For sticking around and being here for me," I yawned.

"I wouldn't have it any other way." He replied.

"I hope I can protect you from what is coming." I replied.

"If you can't, don't try. Keep yourself alive. Save Alaina. Eventually I will return." He said with a smile and squeezed my hand.

"I love you." I said resting my head on his shoulder.

"I know." He replied. I leaned over and quickly kissed his cheek. He licked his lips and smiled. "I love you too."

"Do you think we can get a flight out in the next three days?" I asked.

"Don't know," He said.

"I hope it's as easy as you make it sound."

"Now's your chance to try out your compulsion ability and don't feel bad, you are paying them to do it." He laughed.

He pulled up to the front doors of the airport. I turned to Erick before getting out. "I know and I am at the point now that feeling bad is on the back burner, until I get my daughter then I will apologize for anything I have said or done that hurt to anyone." I squeezed his hand.

"You don't need to apologize for anything. Everyone understands." He replied. I got out of the car and scurried through the rotating doors.

Erick was right but it still did not sit well with me. He dropped me off at the main entrance to the airport. I quickly made my way through. I stood in line and waited for my turn. The woman at the desk called next, so I stepped forward.

"I would like ten tickets to London England." I said.

"Ten."

"Correct." I made eye contact.

"Return?"

"Some."

"How many return flights."

"Can that be decided when they pick the tickets up." She eyed me for a long moment then started up with her computer. I started to feel her nervousness. I jumped into her mind. I was so worried that she was one of them. She was worried that I was a terrorist.

"Date of departure?"

"Uh—week today," I replied with a smile. She typed away on her keyboard again.

"Are they to be together?"

"Not necessary." I said.

"First class?"

"No." I answered. She typed again then gave me the total. I handed her the credit card that I got from our contact and waited. She swiped the card then moments later handed me a pen and the slip to sign. I signed it and handed it back.

"They will be available for pick up on the day of your departure. Make sure you are here two hours prior to boarding."

"Thank you." I replied packed everything back in my wallet and left immediately. When I reached the doors someone from outside glanced up at me. He did not look at all familiar but the way he glanced at me made me feel very uneasy.

I turned from the door and dialled Erick's number.

"I'm being followed." I said walking to the next available exit.

"How do you know?"

"They spotted me at the doors. I'm walking west and will exit the next set of doors. Drive down there, keep an eye out for a man in a black trench coat." I said then quickened my pace. When I reached the doors, I attempted to walk out but the man grabbed me and then another man joined him and they whisked me off down the hall through a set of security doors.

"What the hell is going on?" I demanded.

"We just have a few questions for you." The one officer replied and pointed to the chair. I could sense Erick had followed us.

"What kind of questions?"

"Why are you buying ten tickets to England?" He added.

"What? Is it against the law to buy ten plane tickets?"

"No it is not, but only a few of them will be returning, why is that?" The other asked.

"You think I'm planning something?" I questioned.

"You tell us." The man asked. "You mind explaining yourself a little here please."

"Wow . . . I just came in to buy plane tickets for a wedding and some of the guests live in England. Is there an issue with that, do you need to see their Dual citizenships?"

"Who is getting married?" The heavy officer asked.

"I am." I lied. I projected my thoughts to Erick and prayed he was getting them. "Why is this any of your business?"

"We need to keep track of any suspicious activity due to the past terrorist attacks. Is your fiancé here?"

"Yes he is probably freaking out outside the door you dragged me through."

"Why did you run?"

"I didn't."

"When you saw me you ran."

"No when I didn't see his car I ran." This was getting tedious. "Can I go yet?" The one man left and moments later, he brought Erick through.

"This is the fiancé?" He asked.

"You are marrying her?" He asked.

"Yes—what is this all about?" He asked his accent very thick and angry. I wagged my brows at him.

"We just needed to verify that the tickets ordered were in fact for legitimate purposes." The man replied clearing his throat.

"Well didn't she tell you that?"

"She did."

"Then why haven't you let her go?" He questioned. "It is absolutely ridiculous that I have to come in here like this, to rescue her from you idiots. My car is probably being towed right now. Honestly gentlemen, this is beyond ridiculous." He laid it on thick.

"Sorry about this Sir, just follow us." He said and they walked us out to our car.

"Is this going to be an issue when we pick up our tickets?"

"No Sir everything will be just fine."

"Thank you." Erick nodded then walked around to get in, as did I.

"You are amazing." I swooned.

"I know." He leaned over and kissed me. "You know you could have avoided this all by compelling them." He stated. I shrugged.

"Yeah well, I never thought of that." I sighed.

We drove off the ramp and back onto the highway towards our present location. For the rest of the drive, life felt normal. As normal as it should be without the whole vampire-angel, death dealing maniacs out to destroy my entire bloodline thing. I did all I could to block the images of my past from my mind.

It took a while but I did finally fall asleep. When I opened my eyes again, Erick was talking on this cell phone and we were parked on the side of the road. I don't know who he was talking to nor could I understand anything he was saying. He was talking in a language that I was not familiar with. I closed my eyes and listened closely to his conversation.

"Fel canfuoch 'u 'na?" His voice was almost a whisper. *'So you have seen them then?'* Then he added, "Byddwn yn cyrraedd mewn wythnos." then hung up the phone. *'We should arrive very soon.'*

"Who was that?" I asked. "And what was that?"

"That was a contact in England and that my darling was Welsh." He smiled warmly as he leaned across the seat to kiss me.

"You speak Welsh. I didn't know it was a particular language."

"I have had time to learn many languages." He replied. "I dragoste tu." His eyes lit up.

"What does that mean?" I asked.

"I love you."

"Oh, I dragoste tu too." I laughed as I tried to reiterate the exact words. Erick shook his head smiling. It was like music to my ears hearing him laugh again. I knew Erick would be by my side to the end. That's what my vision had already shown me. No matter how much I tried to talk him out of it, he would come with me.

*****

Chapter Twelve

None of us spoke for a week. We stayed in separate hotels but in close proximity. On the day we were to depart, we lost two vampires. Apparently, the council caught wind of our plans to come to them and they sent someone to pick us off one by one. Luckily, before they could kill anymore, we took them out. Stavros activated the emergency phone tree when they attacked him. I was at the top of everyone's list so I received the call first. Erick, Ambrose and I were able to get there in time to catch them but not stop them from killing the others. There were three of them and they put up a good fight. Our guard was up and we just kept our eyes peeled and ready for anything. Moira and Lennox kept our flank, Ambrose and Draven were ahead to draw anyone out. Victoria, Erick and I huddled close together. Exposure is not something they want but they certainly did not want me arriving on their front door. I prayed Alaina was fine and they had not hurt her in anyway. My heart palpitated at the thought of our reunion.

"No one is here. At least for the moment, cloak yerself Sarah. We dinnae want 'em to detect ye." Lennox suggested coming up from behind grabbing my waist and leaning in close to whisper. I was not entirely sure if he did that on purpose or just to irritate Erick. However the reason, it bothered Erick, a lot. I nodded and pulled away slowly turning to face him. He smiled and nodded back.

"Don't." I scowled.

We all gathered in the waiting area for the plane to load. I was leaning on the ledge attached to the window looking out. Erick stood next to me silently. Lennox and Moira were on the other end talking, their backs to us. Draven and Victoria were sitting patiently in chairs next to one another and there were others that also joined us within the two hours that we were there waiting.

An announcement came over the speakers that the plane was now boarding. My stomach began to flip, as I gathered my things and followed the crowd. Erick squeezed my hand as he walked beside me. I glanced over and smiled. We acted as though none of us knew each other, apart from the couples who got on together.

Ambrose was in the back of the line watching for anyone who may attack. Draven was the first of us to board. He handed his ticket to the woman and glanced back at me. I squinted slightly to acknowledge him. He turned back and continued through the gate. When I finally got on, the flight attendant showed us to our seats. I smiled and thanked her as I placed my bag in the overhead storage. Erick did the same. We could all see each other with the seats we had. Lennox walked up and sat next to me. I shook my head as I spotted the glare on Erick. I reached over and touched his hand and his glare changed. I mouthed I love you and then sat back in my seat.

"You ready for this?" He asked. I did not look at him but I shook my head nervously. Who could be ready for this? I was the worst off out of everyone, well apart from Erick who was half-mundane. Ambrose was literally the last one to board the plane. He scanned the faces in the crowd, slightly nodding at the familiar ones. When he saw me, his jaw clenched. He took his seat, which was two rows up from Erick.

The flight attendant made her speech once everyone was seated and the captain had briefly spoken to the passengers. The doors sealed shut and we were asked to turn off our electronic devices. The seat belt signs came on and one by one, the clicking of locking belts filled the plane.

Half way through the flight, I became edgy. There was a bit of turbulence and the hearts began racing. I was the only one who did not feed before we boarded the plane filled with humans and their thick warm blood pumping through their veins. I squeezed my eyes shut and tried to concentrate on something else. Then I felt a hand touch my shoulder. When I looked up, I found Ambrose standing there.

"I suggest you get rid of your craving because we are here for another four and half hours and it will become unbearable." He replied crouching down in the isle.

"Sir, please take your seat." The flight attendant said coming down the aisle with a cart. I nodded so that he would walk away. Lennox was staring at me and then took off his leather jacket but I stopped him and shook my head slowly. I did not know him well enough. It was not something I could ask him to do. Erick was not watching. I turned off the overhead light and turned towards Lennox.

"Wait one second." He replied and raised his hand in the air. The flight attendant walked over. "Can I get a vodka and orange juice please?" She nodded and smiled widely at him. When she returned, he paid her. We watched as she walked back to her seat at the front of the plane.

"Are you sure this is all right?" I asked before taking his arm in my hand. He smiled and nodded. I leaned in real close so no one could see what we were doing and I bit down on his wrist. I drank until I felt his pulse weaken then stopped. His head was resting back and the drink was slipping out of his hand so I grabbed it and held it until he could take it from me. I wiped my mouth on the inside of my shirt making sure there was no blood there. Ambrose glanced back, his stare caught mine. I nodded but he just stared. My eyes danced from him to Erick then back at the chair in front of me. What was I thinking dragging all these people down with me? That thought did not last long, because Ambrose was scolding me. I groaned, then downed the drink in my hand and ordered another for when Lennox woke up.

There was some turbulence an hour away from London. The Pilot came on the speaker, to announce that we had made it across the Atlantic and would be landing in London, in less than thirty minutes.

*****

Once we landed safely, on the ground at the airport, the passengers all clapped and the Pilot shared his appreciation for their applause. We all kept seated until the humans had gotten off then we took our time leaving the plane. The walk through the terminal and through customs took the longest. We all only brought one small suitcase and one carry on so that we could prevent being in customs for too long and we brought no weapons or large amounts of money with us. I was the first through customs. I grabbed my luggage then waited for everyone else. Once we were all outside, we piled into several cabs.

"We need to stock up on weapons." I replied. Erick nodded then got in the cab.

"We should be at our first destination in about an hour." Erick replied.

"Pending traffic," The cab driver replied.

"Right," Erick nodded then smiled at me. "It will be all right." We sat together in the back seat.

"Visiting?" The driver asked.

"Yes." Erick replied.

"Nice. Lovely time of year to visit," He added.

"Yes it is." Erick smiled.

"Have you been here before love?" He asked me. I shook my head and tried to smile. "Well I hope you have a lovely time." He said.

"I'm sure I will." I lied.

I closed my eyes and thought about my daughter and how much older she must look now. My heart sank, at the thought of how terrified she must have been, all this time without me. I fought the urge to cry and Erick sensed my strain. I felt his lips touch the back of my hand forcing me to open my eyes.

"Sorry." I whispered.

"It's fine." He leaned over and kissed me, his hand brushing though my hair. "It will be fine."

Chapter Thirteen

Neither of us spoke the rest of the way. Erick made a quick call. Since I had never been to London and would probably not live through the night, I took in as much of the gorgeous view as possible.

"Beautiful isn't it." Erick said leaning in closer. "I miss living here."

"How long has it been?"

"Too long," He replied. I nodded. "We are in for a long ride." He replied. "The one good thing about all this, is our allies are very powerful." He said with a smile. I did not argue, instead my eyes continued to gaze out the window.

"Do you think she is still alive?" I asked.

"I don't know." Erick whispered then rubbed my hand. "We'll know soon." I felt his lips kiss the side of my head.

*****

Half an hour later, we pulled up to a large piece of land surrounded by stone walls. As the cab driver drove through, I can see the castle, with tall towers and large exterior wooden doors. Is this what I am to expect from here on out, castles and impenetrable boundaries. This can't be good.

"House huh." I laughed. Erick smiled then got out when the driver opened the door.

We all followed him to the front door that opened the instant we were close enough. The woman behind it smiled and opened the door wider. The inside was even more incredible. It had high cathedral like ceilings and beautifully hand crafted murals in such exuberant colours. Cherubs and Angels accented the corners. The sight of the grand staircase screamed back memories of the masquerade, a year and a half ago. The staircase was made of dark mahogany coloured wood, carpeted fully from main floor to the top floor, in a brilliant red.

The woman that greeted us smiled at me as I stepped toward her. She had long black hair and crystal blue eyes. She wore a long white gown and a—fur coat? She directed her servants to take our things to our rooms. Three men dressed in black stood in front of us. Each servant grabbed the bags and motioned for us to follow them. Ambrose picked up his own things and followed.

"Erick a word?" The gorgeous woman politely asked. She waved her hand around so delicately. I could not tell what she was. She had no distinctive scent and her blood did not appeal to me. Erick smiled and motioned for me to continue to follow the servant. I clasped my hands behind my back and continued down the hall.

We stood in front of two very large mahogany doors. "This is your room ma'am." He said opening the door and placing the bags on the floor by the bed.

"Thank you." I replied.

I glanced around the room feeling a shiver come over me. Something did not feel right about being here. The walls felt as though they were caving in on me. I closed my eyes and took a deep breath. To keep myself occupied, I grabbed my bag, placed it on the dresser and unzipped it. We were not going to be here long so there was no point in unpacking everything. There was a knock on the door moments later.

"Yes?" I answered.

"I don't think this is a good idea." Ambrose said slinking his way in. I sighed loudly so he would hear it. He of course ignored my distaste for him being here and sat on the bed. "This feels wrong. We—as in you, me, Draven and Victoria, do not belong here."

"I feel something too." I agreed.

"This is a sanctuary for Erick's people not us. They hunt us remember." He stood uneasily. "I know you love and trust him and quite frankly, I have come to trust him myself however, we know nothing of the people or this compound. It is in our best interest to move along, and quickly."

"I hate to say this but, I agree with you for once." I folded my arms across my chest, "How long 'til we reach the Council?"

"If we leave today it would take days." He replied.

"But I thought we had to make several stops to speak with the covens along the way?" I asked.

"No one will help us Sarah. We will go into this battle alone." He replied angrily.

"No one else seems to think that."

"I will bet my life on it. In the end, when we are finally face to face with the council, we will be on our own or you will." He walked towards the door. "Telling everybody about it will just give the council more power." He walked out. I stood there speechless. Was Ambrose right or was this his way of getting me alone again. Either way, we were sticking to the plan, whether Ambrose approved of it or not.

He was not himself though, that I knew for sure. Since we killed each other, things between us have not been the same. I believed we were still connected. Only because I can sense him around but something was missing.

The sun was setting and I could see it perfectly well lying on the bed. Everything about this day and this trip seemed so surreal to me. She was so close now but still I felt as though she was even farther from my reach. The clock on the fireplace read seven-thirty. I wondered how long it would be until we were on our way to find Alaina. There was a soft knock at the door. I sat up to see who it was as I told them to enter. Victoria entered and joined me on the bed wrapping her arms around me.

"I'm so terribly sorry that it has come to this. We will stand by you the entire way." She said caressing my face the way a mother would to her daughter.

"Thank you." I whispered, afraid my voice would break and I would cry. Draven entered the room and neither of them looked happy. "What's . . . wrong?"

"I'm sorry Sarah, the council has been alerted of our arrival." He said, but without another word. I dashed out of the room. Ambrose was leaning on the railing in the hall. He was staring at the people downstairs.

"What's going on?" I asked.

"The hunters are gathering. I have no idea where Erick is. I would like to tell him that I am leaving now."

"Why, just wait."

"Sarah, are you daft?" He tapped my temple. "We are in a house full of Hunters—vampire hunters. Not a good combination Chère. We are outnumbered just by the looks of the group downstairs."

"You fear nothing. I don't believe you are worried."

"I'm not worried about me, I am worried about you." He scowled and walked away. I glanced away frustrated.

Where was Erick?

Draven joined me moments later. "He is right unfortunately. We cannot stay. If this is who is joining us we could very well be in more danger. We just can't chance the loyalty the hunters have to their own regimen." He backed away from the railing. "I understand you trust Erick, but these people have no loyalty to us."

I nodded and then walked down the stairs.

"Where is Erick?" I asked.

"He is with Sasha."

"Where are they?" I asked trying hard not to roll my eyes.

"Busy, who are you?"

"I am Sarah, and I need to speak with them."

"When they are done—" he attempted to finish saying.

"No—now," I crossed my arms.

The servant walked towards me and motioned for me to follow him. The hunter watched and glared at me, as I walked away.

"How far are they?" I asked following him through several halls and making many turns. When I glanced out the window, I noticed that we were on the side of the castle that leads towards the towers. I held my arms tightly. He stopped at the door then pointed to it and walked away. I inched closer wanting to hear what was going on. There were no voices at first. I closed my eyes and concentrated and heard the woman Sasha, speak.

"I know that you are in love with her Erick but this is ridiculous." She whined.

"I understand the predicament darling but, this was the only way—even though it did not work."

"Darling! Please do not address me as so. You lost that privilege the moment you chose that thing over me." She hissed.

"Sasha—I am not going to debate with you."

"Bottom line Erick, I cannot have a house full of vampires. My hunters are on edge. You must ask them to leave. I thought that you were only bringing the girl. If I had known how many—I would have—" She stopped talking the moment I entered the room. They were standing so close and Erick had her hands in his. I did not like the way she looked at me. I slowly walked towards Erick who already sensed my anger.

"What is the problem?" I asked even though I knew.

"We must leave for Paris tonight." He replied not looking at me.

"Fine," I looked from his strained face to hers. "I will gather my things and meet you outside with the others."

"You are not going with them are you?" Sasha grabbed his arm.

"Yes."

"You are being unreasonable Erick. They have stripped you of your powers you cannot join them in this battle."

"Them? Does that mean you will not be joining us?" I asked walking between them so she was force to let go.

"We will be joining you, but only to destroy the council once and for all." She scowled.

"What about me, does that mean you will try to destroy me?"

"Erick has assured me that this choice was not yours. Unless you change the way you live your life I— we will not bother you." She turned away. As sincere as she acted, I certainly did not believe it. I made a sound that was kind of an acknowledgement to her comment then I turned to Erick.

"Shall we?" I said.

He nodded then said. "I will meet you out there." He would not look at me. I did not particularly like this woman or the hold she had over the man that I love. I hesitated before I finally walked out. I slammed the door behind me so Erick understood just how much this was bothering me. I listened for a moment then was too upset to hear anymore. This was Erick's lover before he left to become my guardian. Tears filled my eyes and I ran faster than anyone could see to grab my things and carry them outside.

Ambrose sensed my mood and followed suit.

"Trouble in paradise?" He mocked. I rolled my eyes and sat on the suitcase ignoring him. He left me alone for a few minutes then the others joined. I felt Victoria's hand clench my shoulder then she walked ahead looking up to the sky.

"We can stay at a hotel for the night then leave early in the morning." Draven replied. I nodded and stood as the large SUV limousine pulled up. Everyone piled in one by one but Erick did not leave the front steps. I glanced back and stared him down. He glanced away so I got in without waiting for him.

"Is Erick not joining us?" Moira asked. I shook my head.

Victoria was watching me when I shifted in my seat. I tried to smile but my lip trembled. She nodded at Moira and switched seats. She took my hand in hers.

"I'm sure he is safer here than with us darling." She replied.

"Probably, but that is not what is bothering me." I sighed, the tears had won and they fell effortlessly. She wrapped her arms around me. I looked away embarrassed. I could see all their saddened faces as if they knew something that I was only just learning. Ambrose was the only one not sad. He actually looked angry. Then again, he always looked that way.

"I still can't believe this is happening. I can't believe Chase is dead. This is my fault, Victoria. I was so selfish and stubborn—" I began to sob.

"You can stop that right now!" She said shaking my shoulders in her hands. "We warned Chase to stay away from you. He did not listen. It is nobody's fault. We never expected such an outcome." I fell into her arms. My body shook with such force as I sobbed.

The blackness of night had come. Only a few stars twinkled in the sky, the moon had vanished behind a large storm cloud. The truck pulled over and we all got out. Ambrose came up behind me and I felt his hand slink with mine. My first instinct was to pull away and yell at him but I was out of energy. In the morning, we would be taking the Channel to Paris, then the Euro-rail from there forward to all our destinations. Exhaustion hit me hard and the moment my head hit the pillow, I passed out.

*****

'Heelp meeee . . .'

The voice was back again. Only this time it was not calling out to me it was asking for help. The next thing I see is me, running through a forest with Ambrose and Alaina. No one else was in view but I could hear voices, screams, and growls from all around me. Then I stopped abruptly at a ledge. When I turned, no one was there with me anymore. Then I could hear Alaina calling out to me. When I looked up, this dark cloud loomed over me, red eyes scattered within it. I screamed then turned and jumped off the cliff, landing perfectly on my own two feet. I glanced up. The hissing and growls continued.

I spotted a figure in the forest. It whispered my name. I ran towards it. I tried to call out to whoever it was but my voice was gone. I ran as fast as I could to keep up with the figure in front of me but it didn't make a difference. I could not get a good look at them. Then we entered a clearing and I was alone again. I heard a scream from behind me and spun around.

"Mamma, help me please!" Alaina cried reaching for me. Before I could get to her, a blade pierced through her heart, blood gushed out, soiling her clothes. I leapt to save her but she disintegrated into ash. I fell to my knees crying then felt a cold blade at my own throat . . . .

'Sssaaarraahhhh . . .'
I woke up gasping, arms flailing. "Who's there?"

Chapter Fourteen

Then I noticed there were two strong arms wrapped around my waist and when I turned, hoping to find Erick, I found Ambrose. "What are you doing in my room?" I asked pushing him away and lying back down.

"Good morning to you too," He snarled. "What were you dreaming?" He rested his head in his hand.

"I am sure you know." I growled. "You probably implanted it there to scare me."

"I did no such thing." He chuckled.

"Ugh—why are you in my room? I believe I wanted an answer to that question!"

"It is time to rise. We will be leaving within the hour." He said, his finger tracing along my arm.

"Why so early, no one mentioned a six am departure."

"Six? Chère, it is five." He laughed as he got off the bed. I threw the pillow at him and turned the other way so that I did not have to look at him. "We leave with or without you, in one hour." I listened for the door to click shut then sat up. I quickly cleaned up and showered.

There was a knock at the door. Lennox was standing there.

"Breakfast," He handed me a bag, winked and walked away.

Ambrose was not kidding we were on the road within the hour. I was the last to join them in the foyer. I wandered around the terminal while we waited to board the Channel.

"Why are we taking this train?" I asked nervously.

"It's faster than taking the ferry and less of a challenge then flying." Draven replied rubbing my back. "Don't be nervous it will be over faster than you think."

"Yes but what if it breaks down or there is another fire or—"

"Sarah, calm down, you have faced far worse." He chuckled.

The train pulled into the station moments later and it announced the departure time. We all descended the stairs to the underground. I followed closely behind all of them.

Lennox asked, "You ready fur this?"

"Nope, so not ready for this." I gulped.

"Och, loosen up lass it's just a train." He laughed and stepped up to board.

"A train—under the sea! I'm not a fricken mermaid Lennox!" Everyone laughed but I did not find it funny at all.

*****

Two hours and thirty-five minutes later, we arrived in Paris. That's right I counted every minute we were on that train. Ambrose said goodbye and parted with the group. He had his connections in Paris that he needed to meet up with. Everyone waited inside but I stood in the cold with Ambrose to say goodbye. I do not know what I expected from him, a lecture perhaps, about how unprepared I was for all this. But, when the cab pulled up, he tossed his bag in the back and he turned to me.

"I love you." He started. I looked away but he lifted my chin so that our eyes would meet. "From the first moment I laid eyes on you." He said then laughed, "I don't understand it myself, because we're so different."

"Just go." I stepped back feeling embarrassed. "There is no need for this long winded goodbye. I hate you remember."

Ambrose chuckled. Our relationship was complicated. I did hate him but because of the blood bond, it also made me care for him. "I will be there. I promise and so will my people." He said. I nodded. He leaned in and kissed me. His fingers gripped the back of my neck. "Be careful." He whispered. "Don't do anything stupid 'til I get back."

"I'll try." I laughed and rolled my eyes at him.

The train station in Paris was very busy. We waited patiently as the time slowly ticked for the train to arrive. I sat alone on a bench with my bag on my lap. I was worried that the Council would attack when we least expected it. My mind was elsewhere when they announced over the speaker system, that the train to Frankfurt had arrived. Lennox tapped me on the shoulder, grabbing my attention. We all started towards the terminal. When I approached the exit doors, I saw someone familiar, waiting for me. My eyes lit up and I practically reached him, in one leap.

"What made you change your mind?" I asked wrapping my arms around his neck and kissing him.

"I couldn't let you do this alone." He said through my kisses. "The others are here as well." He smiled. I took his hand and we followed silently behind Victoria and Draven. We all took separate cars as to avoid a massacre, which was Draven and Moira's idea. Erick told everyone that once we were situated, we were to meet in his cabin and discuss the following plans.

I lied down on the bench in the cabin. It was just Erick, Lennox and Moira at first. Lennox and Moira sat across from us and Erick was standing, leaning up against the doors. The curtains were drawn. However, a single ray of light snuck its way through the space between the window and the wall of the cabin revealing the tiny bits of dust swirling around in the light. It would flicker in my eye every time the train jolted so I decided to sit up. There was no way I would be sleeping now.

"I'll be back." I announced and walked out. Erick followed me.

"Everything alright?" He asked grabbing my arm. I turned around to face him.

"Yes, I just feel a little claustrophobic," I replied.

"I understand the feeling."

I reached for his hand and squeezed it gently, "I am so glad you are back. I don't know if I could go through with this, without you." I said. Erick's head cocked to the left and he stared at me. His hand reached up and twirled a strand of hair between his fingers.

"After everything we've been through, there was no chance in hell that I wouldn't be here for you." He smiled, kissed my cheek and for the first time in a long time, it tingled. My eyes widened. I had not felt that way since I was human, back on Coffman's Isle where I first met Chase, in the town square. I touched my cheek as the tears flooded my eyes. I was so confused and amazed at the same time. Why did it tingle now all of a sudden? I grabbed his hand and pulled him to me before he got away and kissed him on the lips. I swiped the tears before he could see.

"What was that for?" He chuckled.

"Don't you feel it?" I gasped. He jerked his head awkwardly and stared at me as if I was crazy. As I stared at him confused, I began to realize, that he was clueless as to what I meant. He did not feel what I just felt. He was different. The smile on my face diminished. He continued to stare at me. I backed away slowly. "I'll be back." I whispered shortly. He stood there for a moment then turned and walked away. I heard the door slide open then shut.

Everything felt like it was in slow motion, as I walked the length of the cabin, my arms crossed, glancing briefly into the eyes of the people scattered around. There was the sweetest old couple sitting alone in a booth near the end of the cab and I stopped to stare at them. My eyes filled with tears. That was when the woman spoke to me.

"Que tu vas bien Chère." She asked. I nodded my head and walked past her. I wiped the tears that had fallen. I stood there a moment longer then turned back. I could not deal with all this, too many couples and families traveling for me to handle. The woman stopped me as I walked past her again.

"L'amour trouve toujours une façon Chère." She said then took my hand in hers. I smiled politely at her, nodded then walked away. Is it really true that Paris is the city of love? They can see love everywhere and when someone has lost their love, they know. I had never met that woman before in my life and she knew my despair. I slipped back in the cabin as quietly as I could, sat down by the window and stared out it. However, I did listen as they discussed the plans.

"We have decided that our best line of defence is to get the rest of our covens to join us then reconvene in Bucharest." Erick began, "That is where the main coven is, the strongest as well."

"Whatever works," I said. Everyone turned to look at me. "I just want my daughter back." I said turning to face all of them.

"We'll get her back Sarah." Erick replied walking towards me. Sasha glared at Erick then back at the table where they had drawn a diagram. Erick did not notice her glare but I sure did. I needed to know what really was going on between the two of them. So, I did what I had promised Erick that I wouldn't do. I read their thoughts. Only this time, I made sure they did not know. I listened in to their thoughts as I sat here staring out the window. Erick's mind was clear he was solely concentrating on the plan at hand. Sasha however had other things on her mind, namely me.

"So—what do you see Sasha?" I asked slowly turning my head to look up at her. The room fell silent.

"Sarah—" Erick gasped once he realized what I had done.

"Erick!" I mocked.

"I am sure you are well aware of how things will turn out." She replied crossing her arms.

"Do I lose everyone?" I asked crossing my arms. Then I realized that Lennox and Moira were missing. Sasha did not answer. She did not need to. I could see it written all over her face. I was putting everyone's life in danger again. They were willing to die for me. I could sense that she was trying to block me. She was not telling me everything. She saw something far worse than what I had envisioned, long ago.

"Where is my mother?" I asked Erick. He shrugged.

"I don't know. I have not seen them all morning." That did not sit well with me. Witches were Hunters enemies too. I got up from my seat and went to find them. I rushed through, one by one taking in the scents that filled the cabins. I knew Lennox's scent enough to pick it out of a large group. By the time I found them, I had searched three cabs. They were sitting with the mundane in the far end of the train. I joined them. "We were to meet in my cabin for a quick debrief."

"Well I guess we will have to be filled in once we get off." Moira replied.

"Why are you here?" I asked.

"She is not much of a fan of confined places." Lennox laughed.

I nodded then stood. "I know the feeling." The conductor announced the expected time of arrival in Frankfurt to be less than fifteen minutes. "Come." They stood to follow me.

*****

    Butterflies flittered about in my stomach as the train came to a full stop. It was late afternoon. As we got off the train, I noticed a man in a furry hat, wave in our direction. When I scanned our group, I saw that Sasha waved back. Erick took my hand surprising me. I looked over at him then down at our hands. He started to follow everyone through the crowd. The man in the furry hat turned towards the car and opened the doors for us. Most of us filled one car, the rest in the one behind.

    Erick turned to face us all then explained, "When we arrive, there will be a lot of questions. So please don't be alarmed. They will want to deal with this thoroughly and in their own way."

    "Is there anything I should or shouldn't say?" I asked.

    "It won't matter they will know your thoughts the moment you enter the room." He replied.

    "That's nothing new." I scoffed. "I am a bit— thirsty can we stop somewhere along the way?"

    "They will have something for you when we arrive." He replied then knocked on the window that separated us from the driver. "Please let us know when we are close." He said. The driver nodded then said something in German, which in turn Erick replied.

    "What was that about," I asked.

    "Nothing," Erick said and squeezed my hand and pulling it over to his lap. I looked at our hands again. His eyes forward. My thoughts were scattered. Erick's phone rang filling the awkward silence in the car. I pulled my hand from his lap when he let go. I inched closer to the door. Erick answered but did not say anything. When he hung up, he looked over at me and smiled. Something was not sitting well with me. It felt like Erick was about to betray me. There was a dark presence about him. The driver startled me when he spoke.

"We should be arriving at the castle any moment now." He said.

Something was very wrong. The car pulled up to a dirt road surrounded by nothing but nature.

"Who was that?" I asked turning my whole body towards him placing my hand on his leg. Erick seemed nervous for the first time and it was making me nervous.

"Who?"

"The phone call that you just received, who was it?" I asked. "Don't make me find out for myself." I started to feel dizzy.

"No one."

"Please don't lie to me Erick." I pleaded.

"We're here." The driver interrupted and pulled up to the house. I watched as everyone got out of the cars. I grabbed Erick's hand to stop him but he yanked his hand away.

I scowled, "We are not done talking."

"Leave it alone." He frowned and looked everywhere but me. This was not normal for Erick he never kept secrets from me.

"No!" I raised my voice and everyone turned to look at me. The evil eye was no figment of my imagination anymore. I felt it from everyone standing there. I clenched my chest, knowing full well, this was not going to be easy at all. I tried to walk away but Erick grabbed my hand. He pulled me back and held me there as everyone else walked into the house. That was when I saw something out of the corner of my eye. I took a second look and gasped. Chase?

Erick had his hand on my shoulders shaking me, "Sarah are you listening to me? We will talk after everything is over." He said. The back of his fingers touched my cheek. My eyes watered but no tears fell.

"It may be too late by then." My lips trembled. I pulled away and walked towards the figure I saw. I could feel everyone's eyes on me as I walked past them towards the back of the house.

"Sarah?" Lennox called out. Then I heard Erick tell him to let me go. Once I turned left and was out of sight I began to run.

"Chase?" I whispered. "Is that you?" Tears filled my eyes. I turned at the rustle behind me. Nothing. The noise continued from all directions forcing me to turn in a complete circle. "Show yourself." I demanded. A white tailed deer stepped out from the darkness making its way over to me. I stood frozen, unaware of its reaction towards me. It stood so close staring at me, as if it knew me. I refrained from reaching out to touch it. Then it was startled and ran off. The whisper I have been hearing for months was back.

"Who are you?" I cried. "Why are you calling me?" My name echoed in the darkness. Then I saw him. My name was still echoing in the wind but Chase was now walking towards me from the same direction that the deer had run. "Chase?" I squinted. He smiled at me and I just about melted right there in front of him.

"Hello Sarah." His voice was the same as I remembered. My body began to shake uncontrollably.

"Was that you calling me?"

"Yes." He smiled.

"Why?"

"To tell you—" he reached out to touch me.

"What? You're dead, what could you tell me that I don't already know?" I asked walking closer even though it felt as though I would never reach him.

"I'm not d—" another voice filled the silence. He disappeared.

"No!" I screamed.

"Sarah!" When I opened my eyes, I found Lennox shaking me.

"Where—"

"Ye took aff and when ye didn't come back I—we got worried. What were ye thinkin' runnin' aff like 'at?" He asked.

"I thought I saw someone."

"Oot here? In the woods?" He laughed helping me to my feet. I had fallen and cut my head. "Let's get ye back Lass. Things are heatin' up in there." He wrapped an arm around my waist.

Chapter Fifteen

By the time, we walked through the front doors; everyone was standing in the foyer waiting. Then a vampire in a red cloak pointed to a door behind the staircase. We followed him to the door, he opened it and we all passed through. Inside there was a winding staircase made of stone that lead to a basement. The ground was dirt and the walls were chunks of stone. I suddenly felt uneasy as I remembered that I almost died in a place just like this. I hesitated, a few times and Lennox placed his hand on my shoulder. He nodded and motioned for me to continue. We entered a room that looked somewhat like a cellar. Everyone took a spot against the wall. The red-cloaked vampire escorted Lennox out. Erick stepped towards me and stood close at my side. Two of the vampires in the coven were talking in German to one another.

I heard the small vampire say to the one who appeared to be in charge, "Sie sind nach dem Konzil in Rumänien gehen." The little one then backed up a step and the other one nodded his head looking straight at me.

"It has been brought to my attention that, you are going after the Council in Romania." The other one said to me. "Is this true?"

"Yes." I replied. I stepped forward. "They have my daughter—" He raised his hand for me to be silent.

"Yes, yes, I'm aware that they have your daughter. I know who you are girl. What I want you to explain to me is how you plan to get her back, if she is even still alive?" He replied.

"Why does everyone keep saying that? Why wouldn't she still be alive?" I asked suddenly panic stricken.

"The council does not show mercy to anyone." He chuckled. I felt my eyes flicker and my body burn. Erick pulled me back when he noticed I was about to lunge for the vampires big fat neck. I huffed and stepped back. "They would destroy us all of they knew we were talking about this." He stood in front of me, smelling me and touching my hair. "Come, show me your plans." He held out his arm to Erick who hurriedly joined him. My eyes widened and all I could worry about was if Erick would be safe alone with him.

'Yes.' I heard them both say. My head practically disheveled when I heard them reply.

Wait a minute! How was Erick able to hear me again? Erick glanced back at me as he walked through the door. He gave half a smile then the door shut. He did something. He changed the way this all was going to play out. He was no longer human. Panic was worse than ever before. If Erick had his abilities again that meant he had agreed to whatever terms, they have given him. I ran to the door and tried to open it but it was sealed shut from the other side.

"Lass uns gehen." The short vampire said pointing to the door, staring at me. "Move!" He shouted. I reluctantly followed the others. He led us straight to a room on the main floor, with a roaring fire and carafes filled with thick red liquid. I helped myself. On the wine rack was a tray, bottles of Gin and Whisky, over by the far wall. Lennox made his way across the room to help himself to a few shots of Gin, then tossed some ice in a glass and filled it with whisky. When he turned around, he spotted me and smiled as he took a gulp of the whisky. I tried to smile back but I don't quite think it came across that way.

The two German guards in the room kept me distracted. They kept nodding in my direction, smiling and licking their lips. I continued to stare them down. Then decided I would move closer. In a sultry sort of way, I made my way over to them. Knowing exactly where this was headed the moment I figured out what they were thinking.

"See something you like?" I asked teasing them with my moist lips. I don't remember when I became this brazen. I could sense Lennox's movements behind me. He was not sure what I was going to do.

"Ja, ich sehe etwas Ich mag." He laughed. The other guy laughed with him, then added.

"Warum nicht Sie kommen zu sitzen auf meinem gesicht später." He laughed.

"What did he say?" I asked the one who didn't just speak. "Is he being rude?" I leaned forward and whispered. "I know that you both can understand me."

"Lass leave it alone." Lennox came up behind me grabbing my waist. I slapped his hand away.

"Das ist genug, meine Herren." The old fat man from the seller said walking into the rom. I backed away slowly but my stare remained on the two men. The men left the room obediently.

"What were you thinking? They are helping us." Erick grabbed my arm and pulled me a few feet away. "Those men are human familiars."

"What were they saying to me? Did you hear them?" I asked, not at all caring about what he said.

"It was vulgar, let's just leave it at that." He scowled.

"Perhaps you should go. We will meet you in a week's time in Romania." The fat man replied. "There is enough tension here without all of you." He laughed.

"Thank you again, for your help." Erick shook his hand with both of his then we walked out together.

"Now what?" I asked with a sigh. "By the way how do you have vampire contacts anyway? I thought you killed us for a living?"

He ignored me, "We stay at the hotel for the night and take the earliest train the next morning."

"How do we know we can trust any of these people? None of them want me here. This is not sitting well with me Erick."

"It will be fine and even if it isn't, we are together."

"Are we together Erick or did you sign another contract?" I scoffed and walked away.

"Sarah—"

I stopped and spun around to face him my arms flailing, "Did you honestly think I wouldn't notice that you were different?" I shoved him. "How stupid do you think I am Erick?" I shouted. I did not stick around to hear what he had to say. I got in the car with Lennox. Moira switched and joined Erick.

*****

When we arrived at the hotel, I stayed outside with Lennox. Moira and Erick went to get us our rooms.

"Ye seem a bit unhinged lately." Lennox asked sitting on the railing. "Something botherin ye."

"I'm fine." I rolled my eyes and leaned back. "Can I have one?" I asked.

"A smoke?" He said surprised. Then a smile formed across his face.

"Yeah, it's not like I'm gonna die of lung cancer or anything." I replied taking his cigarette from him. He laughed and pulled out another cigarette.

"I ken ye're upset but—"

Erick's feet shuffled to a stop in front of us. "Ready?" He said. I stared at Lennox wondering what he was going to say. He glanced at me and waited for my answer.

"No not really." I replied. Erick folded his arms and waited. Annoyed, I flicked the cigarette and followed him inside.

Silently we took the elevator. Erick and I stayed in one room, Moira and Lennox across the way. I didn't bother unpacking my bag but I did grab a change of clothes, and took a shower.

Everything about that day, washed away by the hot water. Except for the vision or dream of Chase, I couldn't get over how real it felt. I wanted to know if it meant something. What was he trying to tell me? It felt wonderful to see him again and it almost felt as though my soul had been lifted. I felt a pang in my stomach. I needed to feed soon. The glass I had at the Germans home was not enough. I felt a slight breeze. When I opened my eyes, Erick had joined me. He stuck his head under the water then pulled me to him.

"Please tell me what you did?" I asked pulling away.

"What do you mean?" He asked wiping the water from his face.

"You know what I mean. You have changed. What did you do?" I replied.

"Nothing . . ." He finally said, "I begged for forgiveness. I explained our plan to them. Then I told them that I would not be able to help take down the most powerful vampire coven in the world, if I had no powers." He moved slightly closer. I shook my head. I couldn't control the tears. I wanted to scream at him for making that decision. "I love you Sarah, always."

"So I have lost you too now." I cried then turned to get out. I couldn't enjoy the shower with him but he grabbed me and pulled me against him.

"Have faith." He whispered then kissed my shoulder. I really didn't think I could be aroused at this moment but his kiss ignited something in me.

How could I do this? He belonged to them again and I would be as I should be, alone. His hands touched me and I shivered. I could feel his fingers walk across my skin as he pulled me closer to him and his arousal. I turned to face him, my hands wrapped behind his neck. While our tongues danced, Erick lifted me up against the shower wall. The instant he was inside, my entire body trembled. He whispered in between kisses that he loved me and I reiterated that love, many times.

"I love you." I cried.

Chapter Sixteen

When I awoke the next morning, Erick was not in my room. I pulled off the covers and stretched as I stood. The bathroom light was on already when I went inside. I stared at myself in the mirror. My fingers slowly made contact with my face. With all the changes in me lately, I was definitely a different person now than I was two years ago. Pink tears spilled from eyes reminding me of the person, I had become. The monster that crawled inside my body forcing me to do things I never would have done before. Then one thing led to another and when I looked up again, the mirror was smashed and blood dripped from my knuckles. I gripped the counter. Then I lost it and everything went flying around the room crashing and shattering all over. I slid to the ground and wrapped my arms around my legs. I hated that I had no control over it. I hated that I was a predator who had to kill but did not have the stomach to do it, even though I was fully capable of doing it.

I had no idea how much time passed by, as I sat there sobbing on the bathroom floor. The blackness of the sky was beginning to lighten. I forced myself to my feet washed the blood from my arms and splashed some water on my face. After dressing, I paced as I waited for the others to join me downstairs. Moira was the first I noticed. She sat down but said nothing, her legs crossed one arm on her lap the other under her chin as she looked away from me. Moments later Lennox arrived.

"Mornin?" He said nudging me. I slid to give him room to sit. I smiled and folded my arms. The cuts had not fully healed yet. I needed a drink and fast.

"I felt a serious spike in power a few hours ago." He said leaning forward to look at me. I shrugged and rolled my eyes at him. He smirked and nodded. "I brought you a little something." He said handing me a tin container noticing right away the marks on my hands and wrists. He took my hand in his attempting to lift up my sleeve but I pulled away. I smelled the blood instantly and happily drank it down. Before he could ask me anything else I got up and walked towards the door, hailing a cab.

We piled in one cab the others in the one behind us. "How many places do we have left?" I asked. Lennox opened up his map and pointed to the next stop.

"Stockholm." His finger tapped the map. I nodded and sat back. Moira watched me the entire ride to the train station. I ignored her thoughts as well as Lennox's and concentrated on how I was going to build up enough power to defeat these monsters. When the cab stopped out front, we all got out. I waved at the others from the cab but it was too late something strange happened and I could feel the power around me tighten like a bubble. They started to scream and wretch as if being ripped apart.

I screamed but it was useless the sound of my voice, muffled by whatever power was blocking us. The next thing I remember was white lights and then I was in a forest. Catching my breath and looking around frantically I spotted Lennox first then Moira.

"What is going on?" I gasped pushing myself up from the ground.

"I dunno." Lennox replied brushing himself off.

"What was that?" Moira asked feeling herself for injuries.

"Erick?" I looked around.

"You have been exposed." Sasha said coming into view, a blue light surrounding her. "They know what you are up to and are trying to stop you."

"What about the others?"

"They have made it to their destinations, we made sure of that. We almost didn't make it in time to save you." She clicked her tongue three times. "Pity though."

"Where is Erick?"

"He is cleaning the mess back at the train station of course. Seems that little escapade has scared the others away, for now. There is no point in asking anyone else to join." She replied. "From here we go to Romania." I watched as she circled us.

"You don't plan on letting me live do you?" I asked.

"One wrong move and I won't think twice." She replied and then disappeared. I brushed the dirt and grass from my clothes.

"Now what?"

"We walk 'til we fin' anither way." Lennox said.

"We could fly." I suggested.

"I forgot my broom at home." Moira joked. She rolled her eyes and straightened her clothes. "It is too dangerous to fly. We need to lay low and travel separately."

"W-what? We are stronger in numbers—"

Lennox interjected, "Are we, where have ye been?"

"We were ten greater only moments ago my darling and now we are three." She replied. Her hands planted on her hips just like a mother would while scolding her child.

"Fine," I said grabbing my bag and hauling it over my shoulder.

"Do you even know where you are going?" Moira asked.

"No—do you?"

"Yes—Stockholm was my idea. Lennox will go with you." She said then hugged him goodbye.

"You can't go alone."

"I will be fine." She said.

"Be safe." He kissed her cheek. I watched them out of the corner of my eye.

Moira nodded, "Take care of her," Moira said. She walked over to me and hugged me. It was the strangest feeling in the world. I did not know what to say to her and I never got the chance because she started to walk in the opposite direction. When I glanced back, she was gone.

"Where—?"

"She has teleporting capabilities. Disnae take her far but, she can use it, until she reaches the city. If she makes the train she'll contact us." He said walking along side me.

"If?"

"They are tracking us. But with a wee bit o' luck, she just might make it." He explained, as vague as it was. I nodded then started walking again.

"Great." I replied.

*****

We walked for hours before reaching a road. "This is oddly familiar." I laughed remembering our first encounter. He chuckled. "I told you people die around me." I kept a few paces ahead of him. I was not in the mood for any kind of banter right now. He grabbed my arm spinning me around to look at him.

"People don't die around ye Sarah, they're dyin' coz they monsters oot there dinnae care abit who they hurt. Ah ken yer radge an' ye have every reit tae be loove. But ye need tae keep yer rage in check afair it consumes ye." His fingers brushed my cheekbone. I caught his wrist in my hand and forcibly but gently pulled it away from my face. "Sorry, habit." He glanced away.

The weather was damp and no cars seemed to drive this particular road. There was another road up ahead but it curved slightly left. I walked down it, hoping it would take me closer to a main road.

"Maybe we should call a friend." He suggested and ran to catch up with me as he lit a cigarette.

"No. We are not in any danger—yet."

"We should alert the others of our whereabouts." Lennox replied.

"And whereabouts are we Lennox?" I mocked.

"Don't be cheeky." He nudged me. I nudged him back laughing. "Must be someone ye can contact."

"There is one." I smirked. I dialled the last number on my list. He answered on the first ring.

"Are you alright?" Was all he asked.

"How—"

"I always know when it is you. Since you answered, I assume you are fine." The tension in his voice eased.

"I am but—we have lost quite a few of us." I replied.

"Who?"

"Gerald, Olivia, Dorian." I mentioned a few.

"Oh."

"You don't sound too concerned." I questioned.

"Erick?" He asked.

"He is fine." I replied. "Honestly is that all you think about."

"What are you talking about he is my friend. I was concerned." He replied trying to sound insulted.

"No you weren't, you were hoping I didn't have anything that would keep me away from you. I know how you think Ambrose, there is no fooling me." I rolled my eyes and Lennox laughed sucking in another drag of his cigarette.

"Then why have you called?" He asked. I was about to tell him when I heard him talking to someone in the background in French. "Sorry continue."

"We have to travel by foot. We can't go to anyone else for help, apparently they have decided not to join us. They fear the council." I said in one breath.

"As they should," He replied. "They are the most powerful coven in the entire world. I don't understand why you thought it was a good idea to try and take them out in the first place." He chided. "You are so concerned about losing the people you love. Sorry to tell you Sarah, this place is where you will lose them all." He replied and then hung up.

I tossed my phone and screamed, "Oh—I hate him."

"Why coz he's right?"

"No." I scowled then punched his arm. I continued to walk after picking up my phone from the puddle of mud. "He knows what buttons to push on me."

"Ah 'hink we've all got that covered." He laughed. My mouth dropped and I just stared at him. "Jus' kiddin Lass don't be gettin' your panties in a knot, yet." I shook my head and walked faster.

It was getting dark, fast and we were still traveling on the same road, where no cars ever drive by. When we finally did step foot on a main road we could not get any cars to actually stop and pick us up. The thunder crackled above our heads and seconds later the rain poured down like buckets.

"We should stay at that motel over there." Lennox suggested pointing across the highway.

"We have to get out of this city." I reminded him.

"We also need tae fin' out where we are." He replied. I know he was right but the longer we stayed in one place the easier it was for them to track us. "Look at it this way, if they could track ye better, they would have went after us when we got out of the cab nae the one behind us. Clearly whatever ye cloaked yerself wit' is workin'." He touched my shoulder. I nodded and screwed my lips like a bashful child. Then we ran across the highway.

The man behind the desk looked up at us as we stormed through the door, dripping wet. I shook the water off my arms then peeled out of my jacket.

"A room please." Lennox said out of breath walking towards the desk.

"Two." I corrected and gestured with my fingers.

"Seriously?" He turned to look at me.

"We don't need to sleep in the same room." I replied as I rung out my hair.

"One room, two beds please." He replied. The man eyed him then glanced over at me. Lennox paid with cash then took the key from the man. He placed two towels on the counter for us as well.

"Danke." He grabbed the towels. "It's only for a few hours." He glanced at me briefly as he walked towards the door.

"Where are we?" I asked the man at the desk. He looked at me funny.

"Wir sind Rucksackreisen, könnten Sie uns sagen, wo wir sind?" Lennox turned from looking at me to the man behind the desk. My head slightly cocked and the man answered.

"Sie befinden sich in Berlin." He replied.

"Danke." Lennox replied. He grabbed my arm and led me out the door.

"What was that about? I didn't know you spoke German?" I replied surprised.

"There are many things ye don't ken abit me." He replied stopping in front of the motel room door. He turned the key and pushed it open offering me to enter first.

"What did you say to him?"

"I told him ye were crazy and I'm trying tae git you locked up." He chuckled.

"Shut up!" I laughed hitting him in the gut. He buckled over laughing harder.

"What did you really say to him?"

"I told him we had been backpackin'." He hung his soaked jacket on the back of the chair.

"Smart." I nodded approvingly.

"We are in Berlin by the way." He added.

"Yeah I—kinda figured that one out myself." I laughed.

"Let me ask him tae caw us a cab for morn." He turned towards the door.

"Where too?"

"Moscow." He replied picking up the receiver on the phone but it was dead.

"Moscow?"

"Aye, I have an old mate there who owes me a favour." He replied then ran out the door.

I continued to undress, hanging my sopping wet clothes anywhere. I grabbed dry, clean clothes from my bag then went into the bathroom to take a hot shower.

When I was done, Lennox had already returned and was just starting to undress. His shirt was on the floor, his belt undone and his pants hung off his waist. I could not help but notice his amazingly shaped upper body. Every contour of his chest was full and perfectly sculpted. I watched him hungrily as he grabbed clothes from his bag and tossed them on the bed.

"We are good tae go." He said standing erect and smiled at me. I smiled back and nodded, as I dried my hair with the towel. "I'll set the alarm. Four thirty should be plenty ay time, tae get up and oot the door." He said walking backwards towards the bathroom, purposely brushing past me on the way.

"Okay." I replied softly feeling oddly attracted to him all of a sudden. I could hear the blood pumping through his veins and it called to me.

As he shut the door, he turned towards me and smiled with his toothbrush in his mouth, wagging his brow. I knew exactly what he was up to, so I made sure I was in bed and pretending to sleep before he came back out.

The water stopped and moments later Lennox was padding softly across the carpet. I watched him through my half shut-eyes. His upper body glistened in the amber light and he wore the short white towel around his waist. I held my breath so he did not hear me breathe since it was suddenly heavy. He was a thin man but very lean underneath all the leather he wore. I bit my lip and squeezed my eyes shut willing myself to fall asleep. My hormones were no match for me anymore. There was no control once I got the thought of sex in my mind. It was like blood, once I started to drink it, I did not want to stop. I don't know if he noticed me at all but I had propped my head up slightly to see him better. His brown hair dripped water onto his shoulders and chest. He walked over to the window to glance out and while he did that, I found myself standing behind him. My head slightly tilted as I reached out to touch him. He turned around yawning and stopped dead when he saw me there.

"Hi." I whispered tracing my finger on his wet skin. I never noticed the tattoo on his arm and shoulder before. I gulped because it made him even hotter. I bit my lip as my fingers traced the Celtic cross that filled his bicep. The design around it covered his arm and part of his shoulder and chest. I touched it gently and ran my fingers along its intricate design noticing the gooseflesh follow my touch. His lips parted and he watched me. I noticed his chest moved faster and faster, the closer I came to him.

"Sarah." He whispered and my body tingled all over. My eyes flutter at the sound of my name coming from his mouth. He gulped and backed away. "I—"

"Shhh—" My finger pressed lightly on his lips. My hands slid up his wet chest and into his hair. His tongue slipped out quickly moistening his perfectly shaped cupids bow. I pulled him to me. I was hungry and not just for blood. Then I felt him pull away.

"No Lass." He whispered gently holding my arms. "I cannae." I was mortified.

Did I read his signals wrong? Was I foolish to assume he wanted me? My eyes welled and I backed away quickly before he saw me cry. I went straight to the bathroom locking the door. I paced the room trying to calm myself down before walking back into the other room.

I contemplated apologizing, so that it did not seem so stupid that I did that, but I could not look at him, not now. I listened for him to get into bed then waited a while longer before opening the door. It was an hour later when it fell silent in the other room. Without making a sound, I opened the door and crawled into bed.

"I'm sorry Lass." He said the instant I was in the bed. I cringed and covered my face with the sheet.

Why was he apologizing? My heart swooned.

"Whatever it was nothing." I said rather short. I am sure I sounded terribly hurt. The bed shifted and his hand touched my shoulder. Without moving, I asked what he wanted.

"Ah know that ye are under a lot ay stress—"

"Go to bed Lennox." I groaned squeezing my eyes shut.

"Nae, I want ye tae ken somethin'."

"I don't want to hear it." I said angrily.

"Aye ye do." He replied. I spun around to face him. His beautiful eyes glistened as they bore into mine.

"What could you possibly say to me that would make me feel better right now?" I cried. "I feel terrible and not because you rejected me but because I even tried." I covered my face.

"Ah never meant tae reject ye, was surprised actually." He leaned on his elbow towards me. "Ah am quite taken by ye lass but, ye heart isnae here. Ah ken what ever happened here would only be what happened here, naethin' mair."

"Oh." Now I felt like an even bigger ass. I averted my eyes because looking up at him was killing me, and not because I was embarrassed because I still wanted him. I could smell the blood pumping faster and faster through his veins the closer he moved towards me. I could feel his strong desire for me. However, he was right. My heart was elsewhere, and if we did anything tonight, it would be meaningless.

"I need to feed," I replied. "That's the problem."

"Then we shall remedy that."

"No. I will find something tomorrow, before we get on the train." My cold fingers gently pushed against his chest. They lingered there longer than they needed to but the warmth of his skin excited me. "Good night." I quickly turned away. Then he grabbed me and held me against his chest. I could feel his breath on my skin.

"I want ye so bad right now." His voice shook. "I'm daein' all I can—to contain it." I twisted the sheets tight in my hand. My forehead rested on his shoulder. His fingers tickled up my arm and his lips very lightly kissed my shoulder. Pulling away was the hardest thing to do at that very moment but I managed to do it. I had already connected us when I drank from him on the plane, more blood would make it worse.

"You're right. Forgive me." Tears filled my eyes.

"There's naethin' tae forgive." He whispered then leaned over me slightly to kiss me on the lips. I wanted to give in so bad but I fought it with every ounce of sanity I had left. He gently stroked my cheek then turned away. The bed shifted, he got off and I heard him slip back into the other bed. I glanced at the clock on the nightstand. It read twelve o'clock, four more hours to go. I sighed and shut my eyes.

Chapter Seventeen

The alarm clock went off at four thirty, as it was set to do. I slowly turned over onto my side and noticed that Lennox was not there. I lifted myself up on my elbow and scanned the room in the dark. Over my shoulder, I could see a light on in the bathroom. I pulled the sheets off and padded across the carpet to the bathroom door. I gently knocked and then door opened. I poked my head in and found Lennox sitting on the tub edge, his head in his hands.

"What's wrong?" I asked panic stricken, stepping into the room. His head shot up and his eyes were blood shot. I crossed my arms suddenly feeling very cold. He shook his head and buried his face in his hands again. I did not want to read his thoughts but he was not saying anything and it was worrying me. I knelt down in front of him, my hands on his knee.

"What happened?" I asked my voice soft and gentle. He wiped the tears from his face with one hand, while the other hand accepted mine.

"She didn't make it." He choked.

"Who? Moira? What—how do you know she didn't make it?" I asked.

"She left me a message. She said that they were on her trail and if she didn't call back within the hour then they had gotten her." He cried.

"I—I'm so sorry Len." I reached up and touched his face. I pulled him close and hugged him tight. "Were you in love with her?" I asked thinking it was a natural question.

"Nae—" He said angrily, "she was practically ma mother." He laughed shaking his head. "She was the only woman that accepted me the way ma birth mother should have." I did not know what to say. What could I say to comfort him? I only found out a year ago that the people I called mom and dad were not my real parents. I was still in denial about the whole thing. Now, I would never get the chance to know my real mother. I started to panic. My heart was racing and I jumped to my feet. I paced the room a few times. I walked out and started to get dressed. Lennox came out of the bathroom and stood there watching me.

"What'r ye doin'?" he asked breathlessly. I did not answer. I was not going to tell him. I was leaving him here and going to the council alone. No one else was going to die on my watch. I did not even grab my clothes that hung all over the room. He was not dressed so it was easier for me to get away. I grabbed my bag and ran out the door. I was faster than Lennox so even if he tried to catch up to me he couldn't.

"Dinnae do this!" He shouted. "Sarah!" He ran down the sidewalk after me but I was long gone. "Fuck."

*****

I had no idea where I was going but I was getting out of Berlin as soon as possible. I followed the highway signs leading out of Germany. I underestimated my powers because I could have been in Romania by now, without the train.

"Shit." I realized I had left the map with Lennox.

The next gas station I came across would have maps. I would just have to buy a new one. I quickened my pace, behind the trees. I glanced at the time on my cell phone, five o'clock. I had another thirteen hours at least before it was dark again. I ran until I could not run anymore. The hunger was setting in and I was beginning to feel weak. I let my senses guide me to my next meal. The deer was enough to get me by on a few more hours of running. The only problem was the next time I felt weak, exhaustion hit me hard. I just fell flat on my face and passed out.

When I woke, my cell phone was ringing constantly. I answered it in case someone else was in danger. I answered is with a very hoarse voice as I turned over onto my back.

"Hello?"

"Where are ye?" was all I heard the moment I answered.

"Lennox, stop calling me because I am not going to tell you where I am," I hung up the phone. I sniffed out another meal and then another. I walked for a while until I could smell a gas station nearby.

I walked through the doors of the gas station and the chime alerted the clerk. He gave me a once over then went back to his magazine. I walked around grabbed a bottle of water, chocolate, map and a lighter. I placed everything on the counter then looked at his magazine. I rolled my eyes as the naked woman popped out at me.

"Kam máte namířeno?" He asked. *'Where are you going?'* My phone started to ring again.

"Hello?" I covered my ear so I could hear the person on the phone. I turned my back to the clerk.

"Hledáte ten správný čas?" He smiled. *'Looking for a good time?'* I handed him my visa and ignored what he was saying.

"Whoever is talkin' tae ye, tell him; Ne, děkuji." Lennox said.

"What?"

"Just say it." He demanded. I repeated what Lennox said then grabbed my things and walked out.

"Please tell me where ye are Sarah." He said.

"No. No one else is going to die because of me. I will get there on my own if it kills me. I will fight for my daughter and everyone else they have killed that meant anything to me."

"Ye cannae do this alone. Please at least let me help."

"No." I hung up again. I stuffed everything in my bag except for the chocolate. I had hoped it would give me a burst of energy but after eating it, it just made me feel sick. After puking everything I had in my stomach, I rinsed my mouth out with water then brushed my teeth spitting the waste on the ground. I needed to feed and on a real donor this time.

"Chceš něco z toho?" He asked pointing to his fully revealed cock. I gasped and backed away. Then a rage inside kicked in and I felt the need to kill him. I smiled and walked closer. Why was I acting afraid? I could kill him with my bare hands. The next thing that happened took him by surprise. I lunged at him drank him dry, wiped my mouth then rested up against the wall for a brief moment. Everything was red. I grabbed the body and dragged him behind the building then grabbed my bag and began running again.

By the time I found the next sign on the road it read *'Vitame Vas Do Praha!'* Didn't help me much but underneath it is said Prague so I could only assume that's where I was headed. I looked at my map again then took a quick break. A car pulled over at the side of the road.

"Do you need a ride?" The man asked leaning over the passenger seat where a young woman sat. His English was broken but I understood enough to accept the ride. It was a man and a woman with a child in the back. I figured they were nice enough to ask why not accept the ride. I nodded and thanked them as I hopped in the back.

"Where are you going?" The woman asked.

"Romania." I replied.

"There is big storm coming." The man replied. I nodded glancing up.

Upon further chatter, I discovered the couple was actually running away with their child to Budapest to get away from her parents. They did not accept her fiancé and when she got pregnant before she was married, all hell broke loose. His family lived in Hungary and they were awaiting his arrival. We stopped a few times to eat and sleep. I paid since it was the least I could do for them, after offering to take me close to my destination.

I slipped out back during every meal to grab my own bite to eat. I did not want to chance any human seeing me.

Once we reached Budapest, I thanked my human companions again then went on my way. I thought about taking a bus or train the rest of the way, just so I could rest but the last time I attempted the train, they took out half our people. Besides, being one with nature, allowed me to gain control over my powers. I fed frequently on any creature that dared to expose itself around me. It was plenty to sustain my thirst until I reached the location of the council. Before doing anything to them, I needed to make sure I was strong enough. I needed all the strength and power, to be able to take them out, for the last time. Bucharest was still a few days run for me.

I purchased a Hungarian-speaking dictionary and made frequent stops along the main highway to ask for a lift. I hitched a ride to Kecskemet and from there I ran to Kistelek, where I was able to hitch a ride over the border to Arad. I stayed at a motel there for the night, ignoring my constant ringing phone. I knew it was Lennox because he was the only one that knew I had gone rogue. I glamour-seduced a young man into his motel room then drank from him and left. I slept very well that night.

The next morning I went for a quick run until I reached a small place called Baratca. I checked the map. I noticed a man standing by a truck and walked over to him. I had to purchase a dictionary for Romania and tried my best to ask him for help.

"Cât—de departe—este la Bucuresti de—aici?" I stammered. He laughed then corrected my pronunciation and answered.

"Aproximativ şapte ore de aici." He replied. I searched the dictionary for the words he said but he touched my hand and answered in broken English. "Seven hours."

"Thank you." I replied with a sigh of relief.

"You need lift?" he asked.

"Are you heading that way?"

"Yes." He replied. I nodded and hopped in his truck. I read his thoughts to make sure he was not planning to kill me along the way, even though I would laugh if he tried. He seemed normal. He filled his gas tank then we headed out onto the main highway.

Finally able to rest my head, I let it fall against the window as he drove. My phone rang filling the silent car with sound. He glanced over at me. I grabbed my phone as any normal person would and answered.

"Hello?"

"Where are you?" Ambrose asked.

"Never mind," I said and hung up. He attempted to call me again a few more times then gave up. I smiled at the driver and then continued to keep my eyes out the window.

"You—running from someone," He asked.

"Not really . . . It is a long story." I replied, faking a smile.

"I have seven hours." He laughed.

"We just don't see eye to eye that's all." I explained.

"Oh one of those, I know many like that." He chuckled. "You like music?" He asked pointing to the radio. I shrugged. I didn't really care if we listened to music or the hum of the wind on the car. He picked a radio station.

"What is your name?" I asked.

"Cezar," He replied.

"Sarah." I offered. He smiled at me then turned to watch the road.

He made three short stops along the way. All of which I remained in the vehicle until he returned. By the time we reached Bucharest, it was dark. "Thank you for the lift." I said climbing out of the truck. He smiled at me again. He was a kind man and I didn't need to read his mind to feel that.

"You're welcome. I hope you figure out your problem." He replied with a wave and drove off. I waved then turned towards the wooded area. I walked a few miles before finding a hotel to stay in for the night. I needed to find the location of the council palace. I checked into a room. The clerk looked at me funny which made me feel very uneasy.

"Any special requests for the evening ma'am?" he asked in perfect English. I looked at him queerly unsure of what he meant. Just then, he smiled and I noticed two very sharp canine teeth. How was it he could detect me and I could not detect him.

I smirked, "What's on the menu?" I quickly glanced around with my eyes for anyone watching us.

"I will send something to your room within the hour." He replied. I nodded then headed towards the elevator.

That was weird.

I locked the door and tossed my bag on the floor. Moments later, there was a knock on the door.

'I thought he said an hour?' I thought to myself.

"Who is it?" I asked looking through the peephole but no one was standing there.

"Room service," The voice replied. I opened the door and whoever it was, rushed through. Next thing I knew I was pinned against the wall.

"Shit." I managed to gasp. He held me tight. "What's going on?"

"You came to the wrong town honey." She said. I tried to break free. "The council has your picture up at every hotel, motel and hostel in the city. You will not get anywhere in this town." She replied. Then the door opened again and someone else entered.

"Bring her," the voice said. The next thing I knew, they dragged me into the hall. I tried several times to break free. Nothing worked and my struggling angered them, so eventually they knocked me out.

Chapter Eighteen

Lennox

Lennox paced while on the train. He cursed under his breath for losing Sarah. How would he explain this to everyone? The moment the train stopped, he rushed off to meet the others. Ambrose was standing near the stairs waiting. When he noticed Lennox coming towards him he glanced over his shoulder then frowned at him.

"Where is she?" Ambrose growled.

"I dunno. She ditched me in Berlin." He replied dropping the bag on the ground between his legs, then lit a cigarette.

"So—you just let her go?" Ambrose asked.

"Nae, I did not just let 'er go. She was bloody fast mate. I tried tae keep up wi' 'er but she's comin' intae 'er powers mair than ever, an' there was naethin' I could dae tae stop her." He replied.

"What happened for her to want to leave?" He moved closer.

"They killed her mother." He replied raising his hand to stop him.

"Well how did she find out?" His lips thinned.

"Ah told her."

"Why would you do that?" Ambrose shouted. The people in the terminal stopped to stare.

"What did you expect me to dae? She found me upset. I cannae lie tae her. Hasn't she been lied to enough?"

"Yes Lennox—lie to her. Always lie to her." He scowled. "She's hurting enough as it is. We can't let her go over the edge." He cursed under his breath, running his finger through his hair.

"I think that it's far tay late for that, mate." He replied. Ambrose turned and walked away. Lennox took a haul off the cigarette then tossed it. He caught up to Ambrose who got into a car.

Ambrose turned to look at him, "We need to find her, fast."

"I agree."

"The council has put a bounty on her head and anywhere she goes in this town, they will catch her." He added.

"There's nae way, she's here already." He replied.

"We'll soon find out." He put the car in gear then squealed out. Then his phone rang, "Hello?" Ambrose answered. "I'll be there soon." He hung up.

Sarah

I tried to refrain from moving around too much so that they would not knock me out again. There was a potato sack over my head but I could see a little through the material. I could hear voices all around me, none of which spoke any English. We stopped and everyone went silent then whoever held me, forced me to sit. A few moments passed and a door opened and shut then the hood came off my head. Four bodies stood before me and they all just stared. I could tell this time, that they were vampires. I could only assume that they were the council or the council's people.

"Where am I?" I asked. No one answered so I repeated the question slowly.

"Quiet!" One of them shouted in a very thick Romanian accent. Great the real badass vampires were in town.

"Why should I be quiet? If you're going to kill me, like you killed everyone else, then do it. Don't waste my fucking time!" I screamed. His hand slapped me hard across the face. My head jerked with the motion. I gasped licking the blood from the inside of my lip.

"You will obey my orders and remain quiet."

"Or what—you will hit me again. Go ahead I don't fucking care." His thoughts were easier to read than I would have ever imagined. He found me to be obnoxious and disobedient. I winced as his hand came across my face again, this time splitting my lip open. My hands were bound so I couldn't defend myself and they were bound with something that burned my wrists. My tongue darted out to lick up the blood that trickled from the wound.

"I will slowly break every bone in your body if you continue to disobey me." He replied.

"What do you want?" I asked.

"Why are you here?" He asked.

"To kill you," I replied.

"Kill me, what makes you think you will live long enough to even attempt to kill me?" He chortled.

"Because I won't have to use my bare hands to do it," I smiled.

"So I hear . . . You are very brave. I'll give you that but I do not understand why you are here to kill me. Do we know each other?" He asked.

"My name is Sarah . . . ring a bell?" I replied. He shook his head and glanced over at the others.

"Should I know your name?" He replied walking around me.

"I would hope so, you killed everyone that I love and you have my daughter as you're prisoner." I retorted.

"I did no such thing and I have no one's daughter as my prisoner. If anyone's daughter is with me, it is of her own free will." He chuckled.

"I—I don't understand—are you not the council?" I asked confused.

"No." He barked a laugh, "what makes you think I am the council?"

"Why did you kidnap me then?"

"You are in my town. I always make sure I know who is coming and going unannounced." He replied. The other vampire with him pulled him aside whispered something then stepped back with his phone at his ear.

"You are the girl who plans to take out the council, so I have been informed." He chuckled. "You are a brave soul. No one in history has ever tried to go against the council."

"So I've been told." I licked the blood on my lip.

"What makes you think you can win?" He asked.

"My visions," I replied.

He stared at me a long time then nodded and walked around me. The sound of a switchblade came from behind me and I started to panic. Then he cut my hands loose. I craned my neck to look back at him.

"What's going on?"

"Follow me." He said opening the door. I followed him through several corridors, silently.

We reached an elevator, he pressed the button and we waited. When the doors opened, he held them open, motioning for me to get in. Then he stepped in and pressed the ground level floor.   I figured we must have been in the hotel but when they opened again, we were not on the main floor of the hotel. He stepped out waited for me to join him then started walking again.

"Where are we?" I asked.

"Someone is here to pick you up." He replied and then a door opened spilling the room with white light.

"Shit." I gasped turning away as Ambrose and Lennox entered.

"Nice to see you too," Ambrose replied shaking the man's hand. "Thanks again Mihai." He smiled. "We shall see you in a few days?" He reassured. Mihai nodded then saluted me as he walked away. Ambrose grabbed my arm roughly.

"Let me go." I tried to break free.

"No—" Once we were outside he began shouting at me, "are you crazy going off on your own. You could have been killed."

"So what, I don't care anymore."

"Shut up." He growled and dragged me to the car. He tossed me in the back and ordered Lennox to sit with me. I opened the door on the other side and attempted to get out. I wrestled a little with Ambrose but couldn't win and people were starting to stare. "Do not embarrass me in front of my people." He pointed to the back seat. Lennox had already gotten in. I climbed in, crossed my arms and sat as far away as I could.

Where was Erick during all this? He had not shown up once, since our last encounter in England. I wondered if he had done something to me, the way he had in the past. Like make me forget him because until this very moment, I had not really thought of him.

"Have you heard from Erick?" I asked.

"Yes."

"Oh—what did he say?"

"That he will be there tomorrow, as will we."

"Did you contact him or—"

"Forget about him Sarah, he is out of reach now. He has accepted his fate and he must stay away from you."

"What?"

"Sorry Chère. It is what it is." He shrugged.

I did not respond. I just curled up against the door and stared out the window. I did not understand why Erick would do this. We were finally able to be together, the way we had wanted and then he goes and becomes an Angel again. Tears filled my eyes but I wiped them away before anyone could see.

When we arrived at the hotel, Ambrose instructed Lennox to glamour a new image for me. Something only witches were capable of doing. I looked at myself in the mirror. I needed to learn that trick. Maybe that would prevent Ambrose from finding me.

"Won't work—don't even try." Ambrose said walking ahead of us. I smiled from ear to ear. Lennox took my arm in his. Once we reached the penthouse suite, I sensed Draven and Victoria had arrived. I ran into

Victoria's arms thrilled that they were alright. Then Draven smiled and hugged me.

"I am so happy you both are safe." I cried.

"Europe is the one place we don't have to worry about enemies." He replied.

"Doing this, with me, will give you many in the end." I embraced them again.

"I don't believe it will. It is time the council was re-elected." Draven smiled. I took a seat on the armchair and waited until the room quieted down. Ambrose was the first to speak.

"My people on the inside cannot give me any definite answers as to Alaina's well-being. They are being watched very carefully and no one outside of the elder circle knows anything."

"So we are going in blindly?" One of the vampires asked.

"Yes."

"I did not realize this was a suicide mission Ambrose." He scoffed. "Had I of known you didn't know if the girl was alive, I would have made a better choice—"

"Then leave." I snapped standing up. My body filled with rage instantly.

"Excuse me!" He hissed.

Ambrose glared at me but I ignored him.

"What I was about to say was—I would have made a better choice in my backup." He continued.

"Speak when spoken too." Ambrose growled pointing at the chair for me to sit down. He looked back at the vampire that was talking. "It is unfortunate that we cannot have more numbers in time for the battle. However, we are going in anyway. We want to take out the council as quickly as possible. Their way of thinking, is very old and we need to modernize it, for the future. Many humans know of us, whether they believe in us is unclear but we cannot hide forever." He stated. "Especially when our kind falls so easily in love with the enemy," He glanced briefly at me. I bit my tongue to prevent an argument.

"Speak for yourself Ambrose." The vampire chided.

"I am, as well as for a few others I know." He replied, "Draven can speak first hand, of falling in love with a mortal. Only to be punished for it and now look at them." He pointed and we all stared admiringly. "Together for all eternity and they are happy. What is wrong with that?" He pointed at them. "Then there is Alyshia and Klaus, been together for centuries and he was mortal when she fell in love. If the one we love is willing then why is it forbidden?"

"Because there is always that slight chance, that when the one we love finds out, what we really are, they won't want what we offer." I replied glancing up from my tapping fingers.

"How often has one turned down living forever?" Ambrose asked.

"If you had come to me before Chase had and offered it to me. I would have said no." I replied leaning forward on my knees.

His lip twitched and he turned away then chided, "One silly mortal, of out how many?"

"No, there are many out there that think like me—" Ambrose interjected.

"What if Erick had offered it or Lennox?" He growled. I looked away from his angry eyes.

"I—I," I whispered. Lennox's eyes widened.

"That's what I thought . . . You only refuse me, because of our first encounter. If you had known me under different circumstances the offer would have been accepted." Ambrose was so angry at my questioning him.

"Perhaps—"

"Not perhaps—it is a fact!" He shouted. Ambrose did not take lightly to my rejection, especially with his people in the room.

"Get on with it Ambrose." One of the other vampires sighed crossing his arms.

He calmed himself, turned his back to me and continued, "I think in light of the upcoming events. If we win, we can elect new council members and build that on a new foundation for our people. The possibilities could be endless."

"You should have been a politician Ambrose, no one likes you already." I jumped up from my chair and just as I attempted to walk away, he grabbed me by the throat. The others clicked their tongues at me. Already I have made international enemies.

"Leave us!" He shouted at everyone.

"If she cannot be controlled Ambrose, we will back out." One of the other vampires said. Everyone left the suite apart from Draven and Victoria, who practically had to drag Lennox out of the room. Once we were alone Ambrose started shouting at me. "You insolent little girl! I will not have you ridicule me or demean me in front of my people. I am here to help you. I would appreciate a little fucking gratitude." He said and let go.

"Oh I'm sorry I didn't realize that I was giving the impression that you weren't a nice person." I rolled my eyes and stepped away.

"You know what Sarah. I am sick and tired of trying to prove to you that I am not your enemy here. We are on the same side. I am not asking you to love me, because we both know you are incapable of that but I ask that you accept me for who I am and what I am to you."

"Good luck with that." I replied and walked out. I do not know why Ambrose bothered. I could not accept him for anything other than the monster that made me what I am today. If he died, I would not shed a single tear. I slammed the door to my room and flopped on the bed. Not even seconds had passed that someone was banging on the door.

"Who is it?" I groaned.

"It's Lennox." He replied. I got off the bed and stomped my way over to the door like an insolent child.

"What now?" I asked walking away once he entered.

"Naethin', I'm stayin' here." He replied.

"What—why?" I asked flopping back on to the bed.

"Well first off, ye took off on me last time an' second, Ambrose practically demanded it." He shrugged and sat on the armchair by the window. "Min' if I smoke?"

"It's not like it will kill me." I replied rolling onto my back.

"Ye know lass, ye make this harder than it needs tae be." He replied. Smoke billowing from his mouth.

"How do you figure?" I leaned up on my elbows.

"Well like I said earlier, we are here fur ye. Ye don't need tae be daein' this alone." He inhaled again. As he spoke, the smoke seeped out. "Whether ye like it or not, we care abit ye." He replied. I fell back and stared at the ceiling. This sucked.

"What if after all this, nothing changes and the council wins? What if I get all these people killed and the council dies then what?" I rubbed my forehead.

"You cannae be thinking like that."

"Why not? They ruined my life, so did Ambrose. Him in control—that's all I need." I scoffed.

"I'm sure 'hings will turn out bet'er than ye 'hink."

I turned away from him and said, "I'm going to bed."

"Night," He said and I could tell he was smiling. "You'll need the rest."

"Actually can you teach me that glamour disguise thing?" I asked rolling back over.

"Sure, it's not an easy 'hing to learn but you're a quick study." He walked over to the bed and sat down. The cigarette hung from the side of his mouth. He held his hands near my face, closed his eyes and whispered something. When I leaned over to look in the mirror, I was myself again.

"So how do I do it?" I asked.

Lennox explained to me what to do. I placed my hands near his face, repeated the phrase three times. Envisioned someone I wanted to change him to then closed it with, so mote it be. When I opened my eyes to look at him, it didn't work. I tried it a few more times and by the third try, it worked. When I opened my eyes, I gasped.

"Did it work?" He asked taking the smoke out of his mouth, turning around. "Who am I?" he asked. I couldn't answer right away because I was so shocked that it worked.

Then I whispered, "Chase." a smile formed on my face.

"The one ye were in love wit'?" He asked turning back to me. I nodded. "I can stay like this for a while." he smiled wagging his brows.

I screwed my lips, "Yeah that would be great, only your accent throws it all off." I laughed then changed him back.

"Disnae matter anyway, it only last for a few hours." He said and lied across the bottom of the bed, his legs hung off the edge. I crossed my legs and fiddled with the hem of my pants. The room was silent for a long time. Lennox finished his cigarette then it vanished.

"What's on your min' love?" He asked and reached out to touch my leg.

"A lot," I whispered. A tear escaped and I wiped it away. "I have such a bad feeling about all this. It feels— wrong."

"Of course it does, people are gonnae die?" He turned on his side.

"Well, the vision I had long ago was about Erick and I. We battled the council and then Erick died. Then I turned into ash. It was all so weird but I never finished the vision so I don't know what happens after."

"I dinnae ken what tae tell ye?" He replied. "Maybe we can try tae bring a vision on?"

"How?" I held back the sob that wanted to break free.

"I dunno. That is one gift I dinnae have."
"What?"
"The power of premonition," He replied.

"Oh." I sighed. "Since I became a vampire, the premonition thing doesn't work the same. Well—it's as if it doesn't work at all. I have dreams that feel so real but nothing ever happens."

"Well, what dae ye normally dae that triggers 'em?"

"I don't know. I just remember them—happening. I could be walking somewhere then I would feel light headed and faint then the vision kicks in."

"Well, maybe it's a good 'hing that ye don't ge' them anymore, that sound terrible." He chuckled. "Maybe knowin' what is tae come, isnae always a good thing." He added. I knew he was trying to be helpful and supportive but everything he was saying was making me feel worse. Everything changed so drastically the moment Ambrose took my mortal life. Nothing was ever the same. The only bonus was that I was stronger.

"Dinnae think abit it tay much. We'll go there tomorrow, figh' a good figh' and win. Our hearts are in it so we should prevail." His hand grabbed mine and he squeezed. I finally looked up at him and he winked at me. "Gie some rest." He kissed my hand. He got up from the bed and walked over to the window. I watched him stand there as if he was a sentinel.

Then sleep took me.

Chapter nineteen

The next morning when I woke, Lennox was not in the room. Nevertheless, he left me a note saying, I needed to go to Ambrose's suite immediately. I don't understand why he didn't wake me. I was already dressed, considering I fell asleep in my clothes. I refused to change while Lennox was around. I ran up the stairs to the penthouse and pounded on the door. Everyone was already there, in a heated discussion. Ambrose glanced over at me and said, "So it would appear that the wolves have declared war against us."

"What?" I gasped and stumbled over to the chair. "Why?"

"If anyone is going to take out the council it will be them. They do not want anyone else taking the territory because they want it." Ambrose added walking forward and staring at everyone. "God forbid the wolves take over, then where would we be?" He made a sound that sounded like a grunt and a laugh. "Extinct that's for sure or worse infected by their dirty blood."

"Hold on a second here, my daughter is half werewolf—" I interjected.

"Must I ask you to leave?" He hissed.

"Enough." Draven stood. "Regardless of the race we need to finish what we have started, otherwise the council will seek out us one by one, until they have killed us all. We must end this."

"What do you suggest we do?" Another asked.

"We protect our kind, at all cost." Draven retorted. Victoria took his hand and pulled him close.

"Rules were put into place to prevent something like this from happening." Victoria stood forward and they all turned to face her. "We abide by these rules or people die." her eyes looked at everyone in the room stopping at me. "Everyone warned Chase that seeing you was forbidden. We foresaw a disastrous affair. He went against all our better judgement and now, the people we care for have died." Tears welled in my eyes. "I am not saying that no one can fall in love but it needs to be appropriately done."

"What is appropriate?" I asked feeling offended even though I should not have been. I trusted Victoria and respected what she said but it still stung a little to hear that I was not the appropriate choice for Chase.

"Sarah, please do not take offense, all I am merely saying is that you were a powerful human when he met you, changing you into what you are now is not in the order of things. You scared the council, as did your daughter and look where that has taken you. You should not have been turned." She replied.

"Ambrose turned me not Chase and he suffered for it." I scowled.

"He saved your life because he cared for you." She added.

"I understand that but it doesn't make it right."

"I am growing to regret it every day that passes." Ambrose snarked.

"The fact of the matter is Ambrose; Sarah had a child very much like us, because of you." She said, looking at Ambrose. "Yes it is true that Alaina, her daughter, is a hybrid. She has both Lycan and Vampire abilities, making her almost indestructible. They kidnapped her for no reason other than that fact. She harmed no one she was just a child. Now it has brought us to a point that we must battle for her and Sarah's survival." Everyone nodded to agree with Victoria. "We cannot allow the council to continue whatever diabolical plan that they have in store. That will be a far worse feat for all of us to face." Everyone nodded in agreement.

"Then it is decided, at dawn we fight." Draven stated. Everyone nodded. I wiped the tears from my eyes. It was then I noticed Erick had been standing there. He glanced over at me but stayed where he was. I was upset enough that I did not feel like hearing his rejection excuse. I left the room while everyone spoke of what was to come. My room was the safest place for me at this moment. I stood on the balcony for some much needed fresh air. I wasn't out there for five minutes when Lennox arrived. He didn't say anything at first but I could smell him approach.

"Still on guard duty?" I sighed.

He snickered, "Nae, I noticed ye left unhappy. Just checkin' up on ye is aw." He leaned on the railing.

"You guessed right." I scoffed shaking my head.

"Dae ye feel ready fur this tomorrow?" He asked.

"Nope," I sighed and turned around to face him. "I honestly don't know what I feel ready for. I feel like I am going crazy and this is going to be for nothing." I replied and turned towards him leaning on one arm. "All I want is my daughter back. If they do that, then I will just leave. She did nothing wrong. It isn't fair that they took her." I started to cry.

"It's gonnae be aw reit lass. Dinnae worry abit it." He reached up and touched my cheek, his thumb brushing the tears away. He moved closer and I could feel the heat coming from his body. Then I felt his hand cup my neck and he leaned in to kiss me. At first, I did not want to stop him because it was such a nice feeling. However, he stopped on his own. His eyes locked on mine. "I'm sorry." He whispered, his lip slightly trembling.

"For what?" I asked my voice soft.

"I know this isnae th' time." He answered. "But, I just—I needed tae know."

"Know what?"

"If ye felt anythin' fur me." He said. I stared at him with wide eyes. How could he not tell I cared for him? It was written all over my face—lately. When he touched me, even in the most unaffectionate ways, it affected me, deeply. My cheeks burned but he could not tell. My complexion never changed.

"Of course I do." I replied. I touched the top of his hand. "From the moment we met, even though I knew, you would be trouble," I rolled my eyes and smiled. "I agreed to travel with you. I trusted you. Mind you, I never expected you to know my mother." I laughed. He pulled me to him and kissed me. This time I let myself enjoy it. My hands explored the contours of his body under his leather jacket. His hands cupped my face then he pried us apart.

"What?" I asked breathless.

"Naething," He smiled. His hands dropped and he backed away. "In case we don't make to tomorrow, I wanted tae get that in," He replied.

"Wow, thanks. I really feel ready now." I said and went back inside. "You really know how to charm a girl huh." I laughed then I felt his arms wrap around my waist and his lips were on my neck.

"I wisnae sure, ye wanted this tae happen." He whispered.

"If I die tomorrow what does it matter?" I gasped.

"True." His fingers tangled in my curly hair. Slowly I pulled off his jacket tossing it on the ground, his shirt was next then mine. He pulled me back inside and over to the bed.

We were kneeling on the bed together undoing each other's pants when there was a loud knock at the door. I listened for a moment, sensed Ambrose then ignored it. He knocked again then shouted he could hear me.

"Ugh." I grabbed my shirt off the ground and answered the door. "What?" I scowled.

"Be ready tomorrow morning. We are heading to the forest behind the castle. They may sense us but being as they are extremely old, they will not come out during the daylight hours. Unless it is raining and according to the weather, it will be a sunny day." He said, in one breath.

"Are you done?"

"Oh I'm sorry, am I interrupting something?" He snickered.

"Yes and you are." I pushed him towards the door.

"Sure I am." He grinned, but it was not a—I'm happy for you grin, it was a—what the hell are you doing grin. "I think I may stay the night, keep an eye on you and make sure you don't get into any trouble."

"No. You are the last person on my list that I would want to watch over me. Good night." I said holding the door open. Lennox hugged himself with one arm and his other was up so that his knuckles brushed across his mouth, he tried not to laugh. He did not bother to dress. Ambrose took his sweet ass time leaving but eventually he left. I locked the door, ripped off my shirt and went straight to Lennox. Then my hunger kicked in and the heavy make-out session came to a sudden halt. Even though he offered his blood, I could not accept. I had done that before with someone that I cared about and things changed between us forever. I kissed him a while longer until the thirst was too much to bear.

While out for my walk, my mind started to process what had happened. What was I thinking? Being a vampire put nothing into prospective anymore. As a human, I would never have slept with any of them let alone get myself into a position where I wanted to sleep with them! I dated Jeff for one year before I felt I was ready and yet we never got the chance. Then Chase came along and he was the first man I had ever slept with. Ambrose, well—clearly I was crazy when that happened. I am in love with Erick so sleeping with him did not feel bad. Lennox and I just met but I wanted him so desperately and I did not know if it was because I felt so lonely and rejected or because I really wanted him. I tried to rationalize the moments with Lennox to the possibility I might die. Unfortunately, for Lennox, my conscience got the best of me and when I returned to the room, I was not ready for something I may regret in the morning. I was glad he was not upset.

He lied with me in the bed playing with my hair, while I tried to fall asleep. For the first time since I turned, I knew exactly what Chase meant when he said it was hard to be around me. I felt the same way around Lennox. I don't know if it was because he is a witch, as I was or if it was true feelings that I felt. Maybe it was the blood because it was so different from all the others. I turned to face him and we stared at each other in the silhouette of the moonlight that spilled in to the room.

"You are so beautiful." He whispered. The back of his fingers tickled my cheek.

"So are you." I replied touching his face. He turned his head slightly and kissed my palm then took my hand in his. For the first time in a long time I felt safe.

"Good night." He smiled and moved in to kiss me.

"Night," I whispered biting my bottom lip.

*****

The next morning I woke up, Lennox was still asleep next to me. I watched him for a while before disturbing him. He groaned and rolled onto his back rubbing his face. I laughed and propped myself up on my elbows.

"Morning," I smiled.

"Is it mornin' already?" He croaked.

"Yes." I rolled over and hopped off the bed. I don't know why but I felt great and ready to take on the world. It was the best sleep I had had in a long time. No visions

no nightmares just complete and restful sleep. I pinched my arm to make sure I was not still sleeping because this didn't seem real.

"Am I dead?" I blurted.

"What?" Lennox laughed.

"Something doesn't seem right. I feel good, and happy."

"What's wrong wit' that?" He laughed.

"Nothing is wrong with it. It's just not normal. Nothing has felt normal in a very long time and we are heading into a battle that even I know we can't win and yet I am happy." I spun around.

"I think ye are over thinkin' it lass."

"I don't." I replied and walked over to the window. I ripped open the thick curtains and the sun did not spill in. "What the—" I ran over to the door and opened it the same thing. No exit. "Oh my God!" I screeched. "We are trapped in here."

"Ah think ye are goin' crazy lass, just walk forward."

"What are you talking about there is a brick wall there blocking the door way!"

"No there isnae." He laughed and walked through the brick wall.

"Lennox? Lennox?" I screamed.

"What I'm right here!" He laughed.

"This isn't funny. Why am I seeing a brick wall and you aren't"

"I dunno lass, just walk through it. It's probably an illusion." His voice was a little muffled. "Sarah come on!" He shouted. I tried to walk through the wall but it was solid. I screamed and banged on the wall but nothing changed.

"Sarah!" I felt someone shaking me and when I opened my eyes, Lennox was there with a petrified look. "Good God lass, ye scared me half tae death." He sat back running his fingers through his hair.

"What—was I sleeping?"

"I hope sae or we're fucked." He laughed.

"What did you hear?" I asked still trying to catch my breath.

"Ah heard a lot abit bein' trapped an' walls an' illusions. I dah ken whit ye were dreamin' abit but clearly it wisnae a magic show."

"No it wisnae." I mocked.

"Nae need to be nasty." He tossed a pillow at me.

"It was horrible." I covered my face still imagining it. Just to make sure I walked over to the window and pulled open the blinds. The sun shone in. Then I went over to the door and opened it. There was no brick wall but someone was standing there that startled me.

"Are you Sarah?" He asked.

"Who wants to know?"

"Ambrose told me to make sure you were awake and to tell you that you are late, so get a move on." He blushed. I rolled my eyes and nodded.

"Thanks." I shut the door. "You almost ready there pretty boy?"

"Who ye calling a pretty boy!" he chided. "I'm as far fe a pretty boy as ye can get."

"I don't know about that, you take a lot of time to get that hair right." I laughed.

"Well I guess mainly to impress ye." He chortled. Then he wrapped his arms around me.

"We should go." I said.

This light-hearted moment we shared was something I dearly missed. "I hope this ends better than I expect it to." I sighed.

"Me tay." He smiled and glanced away. "Me tay."

We took the elevator down together joining the others. This time Erick, Sasha and a few others had joined. Erick paid no attention to me, as I walked into view.

"There are a few cars parked outside. They will take us as close to the castle compounds as possible. Then we run the rest of the way." Ambrose replied. We all nodded then followed him out to the cars. I was hoping Erick would have joined my car but he did not.

Chapter Twenty

The drive was a little over an hour before we stopped. I kept close to Lennox, who I could feel was trembling under his manly exterior. I took his hand in mine, not laced just cupped. We all pilled out of the cars and one by one, followed Ambrose into the forest. Many already knew where they were going so they ran up ahead. I did not know what to expect when we arrived. My heart raced like crazy. Ambrose tried to soothe me with his encouraging words through our connection. It did not work.

It was a long walk through the forest, down a very large hill, before we came to a clearing and Ambrose stopped. He glanced back at me then addressed everyone.

"I will head towards the castle, alert their guards and then return. If by any chance that I do not return, do not hesitate to attack. If it's blood they want, they will get it." He said and started through the trees. I chased him down and stopped him.

"Thank you." I said standing before him.

"For what?" He asked not making eye contact.

"For being here and helping me," I whispered. It felt like goodbye forever. "I know I haven't been the greatest of—minions." We both laughed, "It was really hard to grasp this new life."

"Isn't that what friends are for?" He cocked his head smiling.

"Be careful," I replied.

"You don't have to tell me twice." He smiled and pinched my chin playfully between his fingers. "Take care of yourself . . . ."

"Bring Alaina back." I said and watched as he disappeared into the brush. I walked back to the group and waited, patiently. I was not sure how long we had been waiting before everyone started to become impatient. I closed my eyes and tried to reach out to Ambrose but I got nothing in return. When I tried again, I felt a pang in my head, then my chest. I dropped to my knees like a ton of bricks. "Oh god." I gasped. Everyone turned to look at me. "They got him."

"How do you know?" One of the vampires asked.

"I—I can feel it." I whispered clenching my chest.

"We must charge the castle. If they have him, it won't be for long." Draven replied.

I tried to reach out to Alaina to see how close she was but I felt nothing at all, no matter how many times I tried. Draven helped me up and we ran in the direction that Ambrose went. When we turned around, we found a pack of wolves homing in on us. My heart started to race like crazy. I could feel the blood pulsing through my veins. One after another, they started to change form.

"Don't make any eye contact with them." Erick said.

The alpha walked forward showing himself. His guards were next to him, all of which were naked as they changed. He stared for a long time watching and observing us. He took in the scent of the area then smiled at me.

"I love the smell of fear in the afternoon." He chortled. "You are one powerful being child." He said moving closer. I stood a few steps behind Erick watching them.

"What business is it of yours beast?" Erick's tone was very curt.

"We heard that a powerful being was in our very neck of the woods." He chuckled. "We needed to see it for ourselves."

"I see—well now that you have seen, what do you plan to do?" Erick asked.

The wolf just stared him down.

"Are you going to introduce us?" He asked.

"Are you not here to kill her?" Erick asked.

"No . . ." He said, as if we should have known that. Just then, something came running out of the trees right at me. I raised my hands and a ball of fire shot out at it. The alpha laughed then shook his head at the charred beast lie wiggling on the ground. The air reeked of burnt hair and flesh. "Old fool." He laughed, "We may not like her kind but we are not here to battle her, we are here to battle what is after her." He said. "To gain what was once ours."

"That will never happen dog." Slowly the coven of vampires, showed their faces. It was as if they cloaked themselves, by a dark shadow. They were listening in all along. The alpha growled then backed away.

"Good luck." He joined the others as they circled around us. The first attack came from a young vampire, who clearly had not seen what I was capable of. I shot him with a ball of fire setting him ablaze; the smell of his burnt flesh made me nauseous. Erick stood close to me, as did Lennox. I glanced around and a vast army of vampires approached.

"Shit." I gasped clenching my chest.

"What are you here for?" One of the enemies shouted. No one answered and I was still short of breath.

"Alaina!" Victoria answered standing next to me.

"Alaina," He replied tapping his lip. "Of whom do you speak?" One of the others leaned forward and whispered in his ear just as I shouted.

"My daughter," I shouted and the ground rumbled.

"Your daughter—oh the hybrid," He smiled. He did not notice the ground rumble beneath his feet. I cocked my head surprised. He continued to stare me down then he said, "Bring her forward."

"Alaina—" I gasped then lunged for him but Erick held on to me.

"I also do not see why we should allow you to live." He said.

"I suggest you shut your mouth."

"Or what," He chortled. "You brought this monstrosity into the world. You are a now a far greater threat to us than before." The vampire said. "You shall both die."

"You will never get the chance?" I retorted. I could feel the heat in my body rise. Erick let me go.

"I wouldn't be so sure of that child—"

"Oh you can bet on it!" The anger rose and everyone stared at me in shock. I was panting and my fists were clenched, blood dripped from my palms. "You will die even, if I have to make sure of it!" I hissed and went at him. The vampire elder smiled at me as though he feared nothing and drove that blade through Alaina's heart.

"No!" I screamed.

Everything moved in slow motion after that. Then I saw red. The next thing I remembered hearing was from the vampire I was about to impale, 'Her eyes?' before I took his life. But as I drained the life from his body, I saw my daughter. I watched everything they had done to her, from the moment they took her to the moment she died. I dropped his body and turned to face the others. A few of the elders tried to run but they did not get far. When I opened my eyes again, I could feel a bit of that anger rise and the lust for blood kicked in full gear. I must have looked like a monster to anyone who came in my path because the fear on their faces was far worse than ever before. Another vampire in my arms drained of all his blood. More images of my daughter. I jumped back, stared at him then set him on fire. I could hear someone screaming but it was too muffled to make out. Then I spotted another elder and went at him. I latched onto his back and my teeth sunk into his cold flesh. This new power fuelled my desire to end his life and the ones that followed. I charged the vampire in front of me with bloodlust red eyes, the elder pleaded with me.

"If you kill me you will never find your answers."

"I have no questions that need answering?" I growled.

"There is one thing of interest to you." He replied. He let his guard down so I grabbed him before he could stop me again.

"What makes you think there is anything else of interest out there." I shouted and bit down on his jugular like a ravage animal. I honestly don't remember what happened after that.

'*Sssaaraaah.*' The voice was back again.

I let him go dropping his lifeless body on the ground. '*Stop before it is too late.*'

"It's already too late!" I screamed. I turned to find Lennox standing there with his hands up defensively. I stepped forward to attack and he stepped back his hands still up.

"Sarah, stop." He begged. I waited for my eyes to focus. I watched him walk towards me. His face filled with regret. My head tilted to the left and I stared him down.

"What?" Blood spilled from my mouth.

"Stop," He said as he pulled me close. I did not understand why he wanted me to stop. When I pulled myself away from his grasp, everything around me had changed; nothing left but charred remains. The council was obliterated and the wolves still burning.

I slowly turned all the way around. My body shook and I fell to my knees screaming, "No . . ." My fists banged on the earth beneath me. "NO!"

*****

The next thing I remember was voices all around me, crackling sounds and the smell of burnt flesh. I did not want to open my eyes. The air around us was so hot. I tried to make out the voices but nothing was clear enough. It was as if I was under water. Then it stopped. I felt an arm around my neck lifting me up and a muffled scream in my ear. I tried to talk but nothing came out of my mouth.

When I came too, I took in the area around me. There was no one around but Lennox.

"Sarah can you hear me?" Lennox asked. I nodded because my throat felt raw.

"Why is my skin burning?" I choked.

"Ah dah ken, love. But, we have tae gie out of here now before anythin' else happens." I felt the wind whip all around me as he ran. I could not keep my eyes open. They burned so bad. "It's all right Sarah, rest, we'll be safe soon." That was the last thing I heard him say, before I passed out again.

Lennox

Lennox smashed the window on a truck then got in. "Make haste my friend, who knows what else is out there." Draven said slamming the door shut. Lennox nodded then hotwired the truck and sped off.

"Wha—what's going on?" I belted out.

"It's okay Sarah." Victoria said embracing me. "We've almost reached the train station." I heard most of what she said but there was a buzzing in my head. It was painful. Then a flutter of images, flipped rapidly through my mind. I cried out but my eyes would not open.

"Sarah?" I could hear Victoria say, but I could not answer. I felt locked in my head.

Horrible images of people being ripped apart, the blade piercing my daughter's heart and Erick with this bright white light. Erick... Tears filled my eyes. He was glowing and everything around us stopped moving. Then the images stopped. All I saw now was Erick suspended in

the air; his wings extended to their fullest and a bright white light behind him. His markings glistened in the light. I reached up to touch him but my fingers touched a clear bubble.

"Erick." I gasped and covered my mouth. "No! Don't do it!"

"What is she doing?" Lennox asked glancing back.
"She is remembering I think." Victoria answered.
The vision continued.

"Remember that I will always love you." His hand and touched my face. "Good-bye." He slowly started to float towards the blue sky behind him.

"No!" I cried out.

"I have done what I have come to do." He said cryptically.

"Why! Why do you want to leave me!" I cried. He smiled at me and I suddenly felt—happy. He blew me a kiss and then he was gone. I stood there alone, with the charred remains of the war. The damage went on for miles. Bodies scattered everywhere, some still on fire, others burnt beyond recognition.

I was shaking so hard my chest felt like it was going to cave in. "Sarah! Wake up!" Lennox yelled. Something wet was dripping on my face. I shook my head and blinked until my eyes cleared. Sitting up I looked at everyone who circled around me. "Are ye okay?" He asked. His eyes filled with terror.

"I—I don't know?"

"What did ye see?"

"Erick." I said in a whisper.

Draven and Victoria took a step back.

"He's gone." Lennox replied.

"I know." My lip trembled.

"We need tae go. I'm sorry Lass. I ken ye are hurtin' but the longer we stay here—" He said.

"Did anyone survive?"

"No one else survived," Victoria replied.

"How did we?" I asked getting to my feet unsteadily. "Erick?"

"That's why he died?" Victoria replied.

"We always knew that there was someone who would be there to protect you Sarah. You knew it was him, you just didn't want to believe it." Draven said matter-of-factly. Lennox knocked on the window of a cab and asked if we could get in, the driver nodded. I got in the backseat with Victoria and Lennox. Draven sat in the front. The rain had begun to pour and the streets were instantly flooded. I stared out the window, watching the people of Romania run around, trying to get out of the rain. Some had large umbrellas others used newspapers to shield them from the rain. If only they knew, about the real dangers that await them. No one would leave their house again. People would fear the creature that lurked the nights. People would fear me. I fear me. Lennox squeezed my hand bringing me out of my despairing thoughts. I glanced at him briefly with a smile.

I still had no more control over my abilities than before. I don't even remember doing what I did. I had lost everything.

How could I go on?

Chapter Twenty-One

When we arrived safely at JFK Airport, a relief came over me. The only relief I did not get was from the burning on my skin. I excused myself, went to the public bathroom and stripped off my shirt. I needed to see what damage the fire did to my skin. When I looked in the mirror, there was no burn at all. However, the hunters markings had spread across my shoulder blades and down towards the small of my back. Even though, I was this monster, they still marked me. Tears filled my eyes as I remembered the markings on Erick's body glitter in the light.

He was gone.

I threw cold water on my face and walked out. That was when I ran into Sasha. My heart raced and my eyes widened. She vowed if given the chance she would kill me. I stood tall and ready for whatever she would throw at me.

"So you live." She sneered. "What a shame."

"What do you want—revenge?"

"No, unfortunately you are not allowed to be touched. They wanted to ask you to join their side." She gagged. "There is nothing they can do about your vampire side but your hunter half, they are interested in." She replied crossing her arms.

"What is the deal if I take it?"

"You hunt your kind down, kill them and make sure they do not have the chance to resurrect. That is all they ask and no one will harm you."

"Is there a list?"

"No. The deal is, if you find one, you kill it."

"Really and that's it?" I replied skeptic.

"Yes."

"Then . . . I want Erick too."

"No deal." She shook her head.

"Why?"

"He died saving you, isn't that enough?" She scowled. "Besides you seem chummy with your new beau out there."

"He is a friend, that's all." I winced but looked away so she did not see it.

"They are not going to risk losing him again. They were barely able to track his soul down the last time."

"Track his soul down?" I questioned.

"Yes for resurrection. We do not know how long it will take for his soul to be reborn and when it does as soon as it is ready to be taken by them, they will give him his guardianship again."

"What makes you think his soul will take the same path?" I asked.

"It has for so many centuries already. His soul is pure as was yours until you took this path."

"I did not choose this path!" I shouted.

"None-the-less, the Hierarchy still finds you valuable, even after my constant argument to destroy you." She retorted.

"Thanks." I rolled my eyes. If anything, she was very blunt. She did not hide her distaste for me. Then that made me curious, was she always hateful of me. "How long have you known about me?" I asked.

"What?" She replied a little caught off guard.

Then I thought to myself. If she has hated me for all these centuries, how do I know she was not part of destroying me, just as Celeste did? My eyes flickered and she gasped. There was no doubt in my mind she was guilty of something. She looked frightened.

"Did you try to keep Erick from me? Is that why he was so confused when he saw me for the first time?" I asked.

"What—I don't know what you are talking about. I have been in London for centuries." She stuttered.

"Doesn't mean you can't travel and I don't mean the usual kind of travel," My brow furrowed, "I know you can, only because Erick showed me." I grabbed her by the arms and pinned her against the wall. I tried to break through the barrier in her mind so that I could see for myself but she was strong. I knew the only other way I would get any answers for myself was to drink her blood.

"No—don't." She cried as I bit down hard on her jugular. Flashes of white light scorched my mind causing me pain but I fought through it. Then darkness took over and the whispers began.

Finally, images broke through and I could feel her weaken in my grasp. Images of her and Erick, married? Then he died. He found each other again and remarried. This went on for a long time.

Erick died a lot.

Then I came along, well the 'few centuries ago' me. Erick looked so confused and lost. She was there for every single death. She was there when I found Chase.

She was there when Ambrose turned me!

She must have influenced this. Then the whispers started again, louder and louder. I broke free and she dropped to the ground.

"Why?" I asked, blood dripping from my mouth. Lennox came around the corner. He stopped dead in his tracks, his shoes squeaked on the vinyl floor. I raised my hand for him to stay where he was.

"Sarah?" I shot a look at him and pointed for him to leave. He did not move. I turned back to Sasha.

"This time I knew if you changed, he would not find you. He would finally be just mine." She cried gasping for air.

"How could you! You destroyed my life!" I screamed. "I didn't want this. I didn't want any of this!" Tears poured from my eyes. "You killed everyone I loved!"

"NO! I had nothing to do with any of that!" She cried out.

"You put us all in this position with your scheming!" I shoved her against the wall hard. "You are going to tell them or I will finish you…no, I will turn you." I growled.

Lennox came running towards me, "Dinnae do anythin' ye will regret!" he said.

"Go away Lennox, this has nothing to do with you." I spat.

"Look at ye, turnin' intae the thing ye hate the most," He cried. "Dinnae let it control ye lass. Fight it."

He begged me. I wouldn't hear of it. I needed her to pay for what she had done to me. "Sarah, don't do it." I tried to shake off this control it was too strong.

"After everything I have been through, I'm surprised I haven't killed everyone." I hissed grabbing her throat and wanting so desperately to end her life. Then images flickered through my mind and I saw myself standing at the edge of the cliff on Coffman's Isle. I gasped and let her go backing away. She grabbed at her throat. My eyes widened as I take in the images.

"It was you!" I gasped and almost chocked on my own words. Fear filled her eyes. "You were the voice all along! You tried to kill me!" Sasha's body shimmered as though she was about to white-light her way out of here, but I was not going to let her get away that easy. "All this time the whispers were you, even when I was trapped in Erick's cellar."

Her eyes widened, "What?"

"I thought I was losing my mind. I couldn't figure out where the whispers were coming from—"

She interjected, "I—I don't know what you are talking about?"

"Even after the battle I heard it." I replied.

"Sarah—" Lennox tried to talk to me but I shoved him away with my free arm.

"That was not me." She cried.

"What?" I gasped almost losing all sense of control. "What do you mean that it wasn't you? Of course it was you, it had to of been you—it all makes sense now."

"Before, when you were pregnant, that was me. After you turned—I no longer had control over your mind."

"But—" I grabbed her by her collar and demanded she take me to them. She shook her head but I threatened to turn her so she would feel the same pain every day for the rest of her life.

The next thing I knew we were in a very large stone room. Sasha was still sitting on the ground holding her neck, her white wings stained with blood. No one approached us.

"Where are we?" I asked standing up and ready for anything.

"The angel sanctuary," She gasped

"Where are your superiors?"

"They can hear you." She replied.

"They better. Show yourself!" I screamed. "Or I will end her life!" still nothing. I knelt down and stared into her eyes. "You better not have tricked me or so help me go—"

"Do not attempt to use his name in vain!" A voice echoed in the room.

"You're lucky." I mumbled and stood. I did not like using her to prove my point but she hurt me. I have been blaming the wrong person all along, and now I can't tell him I am sorry. "Show yourself!"

"Why should I do what you ask? You are the enemy." He chortled.

"Am I? I am pretty damn sure I just defeated the enemy." I retorted.

"For that we are grateful but you are still one of them. Your presence here is sacrilege!" The room rumbled with his deep voice.

"Well if it wasn't for your little Angel here, I would never have become one of them. I didn't choose this life. She forced it on me with her scheming and betrayal." I dropped to my knees, "I never wanted Erick to die. I begged for him to stay away. He chose death. I didn't want to be saved! I didn't want to live the rest of my life as this monster!" I felt the sob break free. "I love Erick and I don't think that it is fair, that he be punished for loving me. And I am certain, that it is sacrilegious if Sasha goes unpunished." I cried. Finally, a bright light filled the room and the voice no longer echoed. The angel appeared. I had to shield my eyes from his light.

"I hear what you have to say and trust me when I say, we will deal with it as we see fit. You have my word that she will not go unpunished." Then the light faded and it hovered around him, contained. He looked over at Sasha disappointed.

"Is what she says true?" He asked walking towards her. Sasha showed fear in her eyes but she did not answer. "Tell me child, for if I have to bleed it out of you, it will be excruciating." Quickly she nodded and began crying. "This is why we banish all feelings from our predecessors. The human world is not for the pure of heart. Look what it has done to you." He shook his head his eyes saddened by her betrayal. He placed his hand on her head. "Jealousy is not a trait angels should carry. For that, I am sorry. You should never have been able to feel this affliction. So . . . For your sin Sasha, this will be your last reign." He replied.

"No please, don't banish me!" She cried reaching up to touch him.

"You will live the rest of your life on earth, with the humans. You will remember nothing before that day. Erick will be wiped clean from your thoughts and you will never be reborn." He said remorsefully.

"Please." She begged. Tears spilled from her eyes.

I never understood until that day what a horrible punishment that could be. It was so beautiful here, among the angels. The moment you enter you feel the immense sense of calmness and tranquility. I turned away satisfied with her punishment. However, I didn't know where I was going to get out of here.

"Not so fast Sarah. I am not finished with you just yet." He said and I felt a hand on my shoulder. "Your memories will remain until the day you meet your demise. I redeem your soul to return if it chooses to. That is your reward for being part Nephilim. I am sorry that this has been bestowed upon you and for that, I agree to your terms, on one condition."

"My terms," I replied confused. I feel so happy that my soul is not lost.

"Yes, your terms." An image of Erick flashed in my mind. "One, you remain a hunter as you were destined to be and two, if and only if, Erick finds his way to you, we shall not interfere." He stares into my eyes as if he has to assure me he is telling the truth. I do believe him with my whole heart. "Erick will be born a hunter as he has many times before. He will not remember who you are, as many times before." He let go. I nodded.

"And my daughter?" I asked.

"Because her vampire half was not dominant, her soul remained intact. She will return—in time." He replied and turned away.

"Did she suffer much pain?" I began to sob.

"There is no need for you to know this. Your pain is great. You can let that thought go. Know that she is where she needs to be, until she is born again." The Angel touched Sasha's head and she disappeared.

"Thank you." I cried.

"You have proven worthy on more than one occasion Lailah, despite your current situation. "

"Sarah." I corrected him. But he continued talking as if I never spoke.

"I know it may not seem so with everything that has happened to you but I see it." He smiled and it was the most honest smile. I felt so warm and full of life. "Oh one more thing, I would steer clear of Sasha. Her memory loss can be triggered and possibly return if you are in any contact with her what so ever."

"What? Why? Erick won't know me but she might?" I replied.

"Erick has passed on to the other side where his memories were wiped clean. Once you die you are given a clean slate, only a few special beings have the ability to pull memories of their past back." He winked.

What does that even mean? Then he disappeared and I was back in the airport.

I ran out to the main seating area calling out to Lennox. I rapidly walked towards him. He was surprised as I was when I planted my lips on his.

"Where's Sarah? What have ye done wit' her?" He chuckled.

"Nothing," I smiled and wrapped my arms around his neck. Lennox did not need to know everything. I would keep this to myself and wait for Erick to return.

Chapter Twenty-Two

We had a memorial for Alaina when we finally arrived in Hartford. We placed a headstone in the Hartford memorial cemetery. Her body had never been recovered, a victim of the blaze I created. I also purchased a plaque for the people I lost. I had their names engraved in the granite then placed it on a headstone next to Alaina's grave. I left Hartford forever. If I never saw Hartford again for a hundred centuries it would still not be enough. Lennox had a place in New York where we ended up staying.

Then, just like everything else, I started to feel— unwelcome. Lennox couldn't move on or at least he never tried. I don't know if he was hoping for something to happen between us or my being here stifled his personal life. Thing was, I wasn't ready and honestly, I don't think I want to be ready. Four men died because of their love for me, including Ambrose. Even though I wanted him dead, my heart still ached when I lost him. The tie between us broken, leaving me feeling alone and abandoned.

Nevertheless, after losing every man I ever loved, the thought of loving someone that way again, made me feel sick. I couldn't do that to Lennox. I never led him to believe there would someday be an 'us', but he never dated the entire time we lived together. But I totally understand why else he wouldn't if it not was for me. Our lives were dangerous. A relationship would complicate things for all parties involved. Sure it probably would have been easier if we dated each other because of the fact that we knew what our lives were like. I just couldn't help what I felt. I don't want to allow myself to fall in love again. Not in the way he wants me too. I do love Lennox how could I not, he is an amazing man. After the war I had closed myself off to all emotions. This must have been what Ambrose was talking about when he said he doesn't fall in love. Until he met me. Tears filled my eyes at the thought.

      The day I decided to tell Lennox I was leaving, he found me on the balcony, of the high rise. At first I never noticed him walk out to join me. My mind was on that horrible event that took place in Romania. It had been six months since the events took place and to this day it still haunted me. I never imagined that I could go on with my life but as the days passed, then weeks, it got easier.
      "Hey." He broke me out of my day-terror.
      "Hi." Quickly I wiped my face.
      His lips thinned and he just stood there staring at me. "Ye're leaving aren't ye?" He asked as he walked closer, resting against the railing beside me. I nodded. He grabbed my hand in his. I turned away unable to look into those beautiful adoring eyes of his. Together we stared down at the busy world below us. Lennox continued to convince me to stay. This was not the first time. But, being around him just reminded me of what I had done. Every time I looked at him, it reminded me of the past.

Memories of the monster that I had become, was too much to bear. Lennox saw me at my utmost worst and I couldn't live with myself, let alone see myself through his eyes.

"Can I convince you tae stay?" He said turning to face me. I fought the tremble in my lip and I glanced his way and shook my head. "I'm gonnae miss ye." He pulled me in his arms. I buried my face in his chest taking in as much of his scent as I could. I looked up at him and smiled.

"Keep in touch." I kissed him goodbye. I tried not to cry. He smiled and nodded. "Take care of yourself." He held my hand tight.

He let me go. "Dinnae worry abit me Lass." His lip trembled as he tried to act strong. I took one long last look at him. White shirt and dark jeans, his hands stuffed in his pockets. The only thing missing was his cigarette. I forced a smile. I cared too much about Lennox to stay. I hated who I was. That was the main reason why I decided it was time for me to go. I did not want the time to come when I had lost all control and hurt him. He deserved better. He needed to move on and be happy and forget everything that ever happened. I reached up and gently touched his cheek. His eyes softened and he held his breath.

"Bye." I whispered. With a thin smile, I turned away from him and walked out, fighting every tear that forced its way to the surface. I got into the elevator without looking back. Once those doors shut, I broke down and cried. Sliding down the wall and burying my face in my hands. How could I leave him? I am going to be all alone again.

The elevator dinged and someone stepped in before I could get up and wipe my face.

"You okay?" She asked kneeling before me. I nodded and stood. I wiped my face and turned away from her. Once I got outside I hailed a cab.

*****

The cab driver pulled up to my parent's old house. I got out and walked up the gravel driveway. I stood on the porch staring at the new door Draven put on. I half expected my parents to come walking out. Then I turned and stared at the willow tree at the end of my lot. For a brief moment, it looked as though Chase was standing there. I blinked and he disappeared. Tears filled my eyes. There were so many memories here that will forever haunt me. Memories of people I love and miss so very much. People I will never have the pleasure of holding again. It hurt so bad to think about leaving but I knew it would hurt more, if I stayed. I could never run from those nightmares but at least I could leave the island where most of it took place. I could not bring myself to go inside the house.

'Seek and you shall find.'

"Who are you?" I shouted into the wind. "Erick is that you?" There was a honk and a car door slamming shut. I spun around my breath halted. I wiped the tears then put on the happiest face that I could give and held out my hand. "Thank you again for meeting me on such short notice Mr. Connell. This is the house that I was telling you about."

"This is stunning." Mr. Connell replied handing me his business card. "I should be able to sell this in no time."

He said with a smile. I took him inside to show him the rest of the house, including the backyard. Then we sat down and I signed the papers. I didn't care what he could sell it for, I just wanted it sold. To be rid of this place, for the last time. Then maybe, just maybe, I could move on with my own life. To finally be free of the death and destruction that started here. I locked up and walked him out to the cab that waited.

"Thanks again Mr. Connell."

"It was my pleasure Sarah, you should hear from me before the weeks end." He smiled and shook my hand again. My parent's house was listed for 1,479,000 dollars, which is assures me I will get, if not more. I honestly did not care how much he sold it for, just as long as the curse was gone.

I stayed at a hotel in New London, until Mr. Connell sold the house. Once everything was done, I moved as far away from that island, as I possibly could, never to return.

*****

Trying to find a place where people didn't want to be in my business, proved to be harder than expected. I stayed in New Haven for that first year, in two different locations. I lasted about seven months at the first apartment before the neighbours started to stick their nose in my business, and five at the second place. I happened to discover that the neighbours snooped through my mail just to find out my name. I figured that out when I picked up a scent on my mail, other than the mail person. Then a neighbour called out to me by my name one night. Thing that sucked about it all was that I paid my full year in advance, both times and lost out on that money because I had to move. I couldn't keep doing this or I would never be able to make that money last a lifetime. Then I figured that if I lived somewhere more expensive, maybe the neighbours would be snotty enough to mind their own business.

Therefore, I went back New York City to try it again and for a while, it seemed as though it was working. The condo was beautiful and very expensive. It was new and not filled to capacity yet. I chose a floor that had only a few people living on it. It was coming up to my one year being there when I noticed that my neighbours would stand out in the hall to read the paper, just so they could catch a glimpse of me. There was this one guy across from me, good looking dressed in business attire most of the time. One Night he caught me in the hall and invited me in for a drink. I refused of course but he insisted on more than one occasion. Then things got weird.

"Sarah." I spun around caught off guard as I tried to slip into my place.

"John." He made a point to tell me his name every time I ran into him.

"I have some friends over, they really want to meet you." The sneer on his face made me think otherwise. I smiled and nodded then followed him inside. He led me to the kitchen where everything looked sterile and metallic. As I came around the corner I found four people standing there half naked. They all smiled at me. I understand what kind of party this is. I glanced over at John then leaned in real close his eyes locked on mind.

"You never saw me." Then I returned to the others taking each set of eyes on mine. "Forget you ever saw me." I turned to leave. I went straight to my room and started packing. The one thing about this place was that I could sublet it. I placed an ad in the paper and a week later the keys were handed over to the new tenant. I made sure I glamoured him to pay on time every month until he moved. Tried two more places in New York, same thing happened. Everyone wanted to know where I came from. What was my name, what do I do for a living. I could not escape it. It got so bad that I stayed in all day and went out after midnight.

From that day forward, I felt like a nomad. Feeding was almost impossible because neighbours were so interested in my business. I moved from one apartment to another, throughout New York. If only I had learned how Chase and Ambrose survived all those years with the living.

Eventually I decided it was time to leave the city and found a place near the woods in Poughkeepsie with plenty of wildlife to live off. My new rule was; I did not sign more than one year on a lease, if I signed one at all. That way I didn't throw my money away. I had to make up a story as to why I couldn't sign a one-year lease. Therefore, my story was either that I was a writer or a musician, depending on their interests. If they were an avid reader, I was a musician and if they were a music lover, I was a writer. I could not chance someone wanting to sample my writing or worse, listen to me sing. I always asked not to be disturbed either, unless it was under dire circumstances. Once I exhausted all the locations available to me within the five years I stayed in

Poughkeepsie, I left that town in search of another. Life as a vampire in hiding, sucked. I was suspicious of everyone and trusted no one.

Then to top it all off my dreams became reoccurring nightmares of that night in Romania. If it was not the whispers haunting me, it was the nightmares. Bits and pieces slowly came back. Some mornings I woke up angry others I woke up full of regret. On many occasions, I woke up crying. One thing was for sure the farther I got away from the island the less it hurt.

*****

Chapter Twenty-three

After another five years, I got tired of moving around so I decided to plant some roots, in the middle of nowhere. There was this little piece of land in Delaware, Glasgow. It was not anything spectacular but it allowed me to stay a while longer, population 15,302. It was perfect because there was no one to bother me on any corner. It was this little two-bedroom boathouse. After two years of living there, I tried to get a job, just to feel normal again. That did not last long. Eventually, I chose not to work at all. The only way to avoid someone wanting to pry in my life was to stay away from everyone. I looked for ways to work from home. I tried everything possible just to keep busy. Nothing worked. I knew in my heart if I didn't find something to occupy my time I would go stir crazy and people's lives would be in danger. I didn't want to hunt just to have that interaction that I was missing. Whether it was for blood or for vampires the hunt was the only current excitement I got. I still had my degree so I tried an online therapy group, which worked for a while, until some lunatic, hacked my computer—then showed up at my house late one night thinking he would have his way with me. I surprised him when the table had turned and I had my way with him. I left that town as soon as I sold the house and removed my website immediately.

Normal no longer existed.

My next option was not to hide in the middle of nowhere but to hide in plain sight, among the living. The only problem with that was running into other vampires. They always seemed to find me and eventually I had to get rid of them. I never wanted to kill anyone but if I wanted to get Erick back then I needed to keep my promise to the Hierarchy. The thing that hurt about killing them was that they never came to harm me, it was for help or for a friend but I had to do my job. It was a lonely life as a vampire hunter. I barely slept and it felt as though killing vampires took a bit of my humanity away.

Every night it got hard looking in the mirror at the stranger I had become and seeing the bloodstained mess in front of me, destroyed a piece of me every time. Scrubbing my body and hair until the blood washed out, on more occasions than I would like to remember. Every week I had to burn the clothes I wore. I began to understand all too well, what Chase had despised about his life. The loneliness was the worst of it. He was never completely alone though, not how I am today. He had Marcus. I had no one. No friends, no real human or non-human interaction.

I wished many times, that I was dead.

*****

You would think that one entire state was big enough to settle in for a long time, without being bothered. But, once the vampire community got wind of me, there was no such thing as being alone. Vampires no longer wanted a friend they hunted me down. Word spread fast when you kill a few thousand vampires over the years. I killed everything that went bump in the night. They never stood a chance because I was faster and more powerful than anything they had ever come across.

It was time to say goodbye to Glasgow Delaware.

*****

Then oddly enough, a year after settling down again, I ran into Lennox one night on the outskirts of Maryland. Two vampires backed him into an alley. He was not worried but I was. He was taunting them with his clever lines. I intervened taking them both out. At first he was shocked and speechless. Then he hugged me. It was a hard reunion but a much-needed one. Time had caught up with him. That's when I realized how much time had passed since we last saw each other. Yet he still looked as sexy as ever, and that accent never faded.

"Look at what the cat drug in." He laughed. He still had his humour intact, which I missed so much. I did regret not keeping in touch with him. His aging, was just another reminder to me that; I would never grow old and never die.

"Lennox," I smiled. He stood before me just staring.

"Sarah… I cannae believe it." He smiled.

"You look good. Time has been kind to you." I said. He walked closer and took me in his arms again.

"It's good tae see ye're doin' okay."

"I wouldn't say that." I laughed and hugged him tight. I missed his scent. Why did I ever leave? "How have you been?" I did not want to let go. I slowly pulled away kissing his cheek, lingering longer than I should have. It had been so many years since I had any meaningful human contact. It felt so...sweet.

"I've been good. Ye need a place tae stay?" He asked.

"I don't want to impose."

"Never," He said with a big smile and took my arm in his. "Thanks fur the help." We walked down the street to his car. "I have tae say love, ah never thought in a million years, that I would see ye again."

"I never thought I would see you either." I cracked a smile hugging him again with one arm.

"Maybe its fate," He smiled and got in his car. I glanced up at the stars with a sigh then walked farther down the street to my car.

"Maybe," I whispered to myself.

When we got to his house, he asked that I wait in the Den. He went to speak with his wife. Well he never said he was going to speak with his wife but I knew that was what he did. I could hear their voices and heartbeats upstairs. He spoke to her about me staying the night. She seemed pretty sincere when she agreed to it. Then he joined me in the Den.

"Thanks again for letting me stay." I said.

"It's nae problem love. Gie some rest, we'll talk in the morn'." He winked.

"Len, are you still hunting?" I asked and crossed my arms under my breasts.

"Nah, I was oot fur a drink and they two vamps cam' after me." He said with a smile. I nodded and smiled back. I didn't believe him.

"Night love," He said with a smile then turned to leave. He seemed different.

"Night," I whispered and watched him leave. I ran my fingers through my hair then flopped down on the sofa bed, staring up at the ceiling.

Why did I come here?

Chapter Twenty-Four

The next morning I walked through the house following their scent and I found them in the tearoom. I stood by the door watching them for a long moment. Lennox looked so happy. Something he very much deserved after all that he went through. My heart stopped when I laid eyes on his daughter. She was beautiful, with long dark brown hair like her fathers and green eyes like her mother. She was the age Alaina was, when I last saw her. I wiped the single tear that escaped and was about to turn to leave when Lennox spoke.

"Come in." He said. He stood and waited for me to join the table. I observed for a while until it was time for Abbey to go to school. He leaned over and kissed my cheek. "Sit."

"Thanks." I smiled and joined them.

"I'll be right back." He excused himself and left with Abbey.

"What brings you to Jamestown Sarah?" His wife Alexis asked as she poured me a cup of tea. I glanced over my shoulder wondering how long Lennox would be gone.

"Uh—just passing through really. I'm heading south for a while." I smiled warmly picking up the cup.

"Alone?" She questioned.

I was about to answer when Lennox's voice grabbed our attention, "Sarah has always been a bit ay loner." He smiled.

I agreed with a smile. I still could not read Lennox's mind, even after all these years. "I like to travel a lot." I started. "Lived in Connecticut most of my life and just recently saw New York. I mean all of New York. Now I would like to move to a warmer state, for a while." I could not look her in the eye.

Lennox questioned, "Is 'at a good idea considerin' yer condition?"

"I should be fine. I am still very young." I replied. His wife looked confused.

"Oh my goodness what's wrong?" Alexis asked. I had to think something up on the spot.

"I—uh, have a rare blood disorder that can be affected by the sun. I use lotion and most times I'm okay. If I forget then I would end up with third degree burns. But so far so good." I eyed Lennox.

"Good tae hear." He replied. The room fell silent and it was uncomfortable for me.

"I should go." I replied and stood.

"So soon?" Alexis questioned. I realized then she was not special like us at all. He chose a human over his own kind. "Thought maybe you had some stories to share about when you knew Lenny."

"Uh—well there isn't much to tell, really. We met under the strangest circumstances and—" Lennox interjected with a laughed. I looked at him confused.

"She knows abit mah life Sarah. All ay it." He said.

"Oh—" I did not know what to say.

"Lennox told me how you battled the largest vampire council in the world." She replied excitedly.

"You believe him?" I scoffed.

"Well it was a little hard to believe at first, but before Abbey was born, I saw it for my own eyes. It was scary and I almost left him but I stuck it out and it has been fine since. No problems of any kind." She smiled and squeezed his hand. I nodded knowing that was not the case. He smiled at her but I could see being that façade. I eyed him then glanced at the ground in front of me. He had just encountered two vampires last night and who knows how many prior to that. Why was he at a bar so far from home?

"Well there isn't much to tell. He was practically my savoir. He taught me a lot about my powers and introduced me to my real mother. "` I stared into his eyes. "He is a true friend. I'm just sorry I didn't keep in touch."

"Oh—" She gasped then glanced queerly at Lennox.

"I told her abit how we met an' that we spent a little over a year together, after the war. How I felt." He winced.

"Oh—" I did not know what to say either. She knew more than I thought she did. "I should go." I felt my cheeks burn.

"All ready?" Lennox asked.

"Yes… Thank you so much for your hospitality it was a pleasure meeting you Alexis." I hugged her quickly and stepped away. Lennox walked me outside.

"Ye doin' aw reit Lass?" He asked taking my hand in his. The deafening of wilderness surrounding his house was incredible.

"Yes. Thanks for being my friend. I really needed it. I was starting to feel really alone out there." I sighed. Tears forced their way to the surface.

"You dinnae need to be alone love, ye're more than welcome tae stay wit' us fur a while." He smiled and brushed the hair from my face. His thumb caught the tear that managed to escape.

"I can't impose on you like that Lennox. If you were not married or at least didn't have a child I may have considered the offer. It sure beats being alone, but I can't risk it." I said. He nodded understanding my hesitation.

"God—ye're still as beautiful as the day we met." He caressed my cheek with his hand. I blushed and shook my head. It never failed, he always managed to change the subject.

"And you are still as charming as ever." I snickered and took a step back. "I love you, you know."

"Ah know … ditto." He hugged me. We walked farther down the driveway to the dirt road. He held my hand the entire way.

"Why didn't you marry another witch?" I asked leaning against my car door.

"Honestly—after everythin' in Romania, I needed tae leave 'at life behind." He looked away his hand slipped from mine. I glanced down at my palm.

"I'm surprised a little that you told her." I winced as the sun begins to beam its way through the clouds.

"I had nae choice. When she came back, I told her everything. I never thought I'd see you again." He made eye contact with me again.

I tried to smile, "Disappointed?"

"Never," His hand rubbed up my arm.

"I'm so sorry Len." I averted my eyes.

"Dinnae be. I'm mair happy now than I've ever been." He pulled me in for a hug.

I gave him a good squeeze then let go. "Did your daughter get your traits?"

"Probably, but I wulnae know fur sure 'til she comes intae her powers." He replied. "Sae, where ye headed?"

"Florida maybe. Away from this place where everyone seems to know me," I laughed.

"Be safe." He leaned in and kissed my cheek.

"Speaking of safe, why did you lie to me about going to that bar in Maryland?" I asked and opened the car door. He grinned from ear to ear.

"Canne get anythin' past ye." He laughed. "Old habits die hard I guess."

"I think it's time to retire Lenny. You're not young anymore." I chuckled. He acted as though he was insulted. "Seriously though, you look good."

"Thanks love." He replied. I held back the sobs as he kissed me for the last time. "Bye." He whispered. Then I waved and got in my car.

Chapter Twenty-Five

Several months later I ran into Draven and Victoria on my travels through New Orleans. They offered a place for me to stay with them but I could not intrude on their lives either. I agreed to stay a few days then be on my way. Victoria brought up the council on many occasions and how their new members were so few. They needed some recruits.

"I'll have to pass on the offer. But thanks. I just couldn't be part of something I destroyed over fifteen years ago." I said.

"I think having you on the council would be a good thing for our people." Victoria said hugging me.

"I don't think anyone would trust me. I have enough trust issues myself." I replied.

"People would look up to you. Look what you survived."

"I love you and all but, that was the worse pitch ever." I laughed. "Besides, I know in my heart what you do will be what's best for all of us." I stated and ended the conversation about that.

On my last night there, she asked me again if I would reconsider. I declined once again then hugged them good-bye.

"You will always have a room in our home Sarah." Victoria replied. I smiled and nodded.

I headed farther West. When I reached San Antonio, I decided to make it the latest destination and started looking for a place to live. I noticed that not many vampires stayed in the hotter climates. The sun was too strong for their skin. I was still young, so it did not affect me, much. I remembered Chase had told me that the older you were the more susceptible you were to the rays of the sun.

Chase . . . My thoughts began to wonder and thoughts of him seeped in like a tidal wave. I had to pull the car over. His face was so vivid in my memory.

"I miss you so much." I cried. This was the first time I had broken down in years. I turned the car off and crawled into the back seat and cried.

The sun was bright and the streets were busy. I drove into town and parked the car. I slowly walked down the strip of shops browsing for anything that would cheer me up. There was this cute little antique shop, with beautiful trinkets in the window so I went in. The bell chimed as I walked in, the shop owner shouted from the back of the store. I had my back turned to her when she came to the front.

"Hello there." She said rather cheery.

As I turned around to greet her, my eyes caught a glimpse of someone familiar. I was about to follow him when the woman spoke again. "Clarissa?" I walked towards her completely forgetting what I had seen.

"Miranda," She said with a big smile.

"Did you have a sister—relative named Clarissa?" I asked walking to the counter.

"A great aunt, why do you ask?"

"I knew her."

"How is that even possible? You're like twenty something and she died like over twenty years ago." She eyed me a moment then her eyes widened with fear. "You're one of them."

"Wait, I'm not going to hurt you! I was a friend of your great aunt." I raised my hands to show her that I meant no harm.

"Get out." She shouted. "My mother warned me of things like you." My heart began to plummet. There was no winning this battle. She grabbed a shotgun from under the counter.

"Just so you know this is loaded with silver tipped wooden bullets.

Clever.

"I—" It was no use she would not listen to me. "I'm sorry I bothered you." I nodded and turned to leave. When I stepped outside, I got another surprise.

"Chase?"

I woke up gasping.

The dream bothered me for many weeks. I decided to keep moving. I continued along the coast. It was far enough away. My life never seemed to slow down though. I was constantly on the go. The idea of settling down seemed an impossible feat. The nomad feeling was back.

I stayed in a small community in Veracruz Mexico, and I was the palest person that lived there. There was no way I could stay here forever. I enjoyed the freedom and peaceful setting. I sent a postcard to Lennox and Victoria. A few words assuring them I was okay and that I would keep in touch. Eventually, it was time to go west again.

*****

My phone rang just as I reached the border.
"Hello?" I answered not recognizing the number.
"Sarah?" The shaky female voice replied.
"Yes." I answered.
"It's Alexis." She sounded distraught. I pulled over.
"What's wrong?" I asked. It was unfortunate to hear that Lennox was given less than a month to live. I couldn't believe this was happening. I only saw him…four years ago. Tears filled my eyes. I started my car and headed back in the direction of the city that I said I would never return too.

It took me almost two days to drive to Jamestown to say goodbye to Lennox. I stopped at the house first, met with his broken hearted wife. His daughter was oblivious to the whole situation. My heart bled for them both. I knew all too well what it was like to lose the people you love, never to see them again.
When I arrived at the hospital he was asleep. I sat down on the window ledge and waited.
"Hey." He said when he woke. Sitting up. "Wa didn't ye tell me ye waur comin'?"

"How could I, you're in here." My lips trembled.

"Och reit, lung cancer go figure," He joked.

"I'm sorry Lennox." I cried.

"Nae—now don't go an' dae 'at please." He sat up. "Ah won't have it. Ah ne'er listened tae anyain. Ah just kept smokin' it's mah fault." He was such a brave soul.

"I could help you." I replied sitting on the bed holding his hands. He didn't respond. He stared at me for what felt like a long time. For the first time ever I heard his thoughts. He was contemplating my offer. "You could watch her grow up and—"

"And I could watch her die." He turned away. "I canne dae it love. I just cannae." He squeezed me hand. I nodded understanding. If I had a choice again, I would have declined as well.

"I can't watch you die." I cried.

"Ah know." He tried to smile.

"You know—there is one thing, you never told me." I said stretching out beside him.

"What's 'at?" He asked, a grin stretched from ear to ear.

"Your last name," I said resting my head on his shoulder. He belted out a laugh and then the room fell silent again before he answered. I wrapped my arms around his waist, my head on his chest.

"Macalister," He whispered, kissing my forehead. I felt his chest bounce and when I looked up he was crying.

"Am I hurting you?" I asked pulling away.

"Nae. It's—it's just—I'm no't ready tae die." He wiped his face but the tears were let loose and wouldn't stop.

I didn't know what to say. Seeing him this fragile was killing me inside. "I want to help." I cried with him.

"Ah ken." He nodded. I stayed with him until he fell asleep again then slowly got out of the bed. I kissed his forehead and started to walk out when he spoke.

"Mah heart has always been wit' ye Lass." He fingers loosely grasped mine. I stood frozen, unable to reply. I couldn't look at him. I didn't want to remember him this way.

"I love you Lennox. Call me if you change your mind." I whispered then rushed out. The halls were empty, so no one saw me back up against the wall crying. Good thing considering my tears were blood stained. That's when I heard Lennox crying and I peeked through the window on the wall to see him, he had covered his face with his hand. It tore me up inside I had to leave. I practically ran into his wife on my way out.

"Sarah?"

"Hi, I'm sorry about Lennox." I hugged her.

"Thank you." Her lips trembled.

"I have to go, take care." I said and dashed out. I didn't stop until I was in my car, where I broke down completely. I knew he wouldn't live forever but to see him dying and not being able to help him, hurt so much. I grabbed a hotel for the night. Decided I would stay in town for a while wait to see if anything changed.

It was heartbreaking to find out the next day that during the night Lennox developed a blood clot in his lung and died in his sleep. I cried all day. I called Draven to give them the news and they drove to Jamestown to come to the funeral. The support was well appreciated.

At the funeral I could sense that a lot of Lennox's friends were hunters too. I don't know how many of them knew what we were or who we were. Then Alexis invited us to her home. Draven and Victoria declined; too many hunters for their liking. Of course I was willing to go for a few hours before leaving forever. I had nothing to lose. I had already lost everything. What more could be taken away from me.

"Thanks for coming." Alexis said as I pulled up to the house.

"Don't mention it. Lennox was a good friend." I choked back the tears. I joined them inside and instantly felt the tension in the air. I walked through the house giving my condolences. After an hour I decided maybe before they stake me, I should go. One of his friends followed me to my car.

"Sarah?" He asked.

I spun around smiling, "Yes." I read his thoughts. He had no intention on killing me.

"Lennox spoke of you all the time. He confessed to us that he was in love with you." He said taking a swig of his beer. I didn't reply. "I can see why." He smiled. I did all I could not too role my eyes at him. Was he seriously trying to pick me up at his friend's funeral?

"I don't know what Lennox told you—"

He interjected, "I just wanted to say we will respect his wishes, never harm you." He said.

"Oh." I replied feeling awkward. "Thanks."

"I don't need him haunting me from the afterlife." He chuckled. I grinned and nodded then got in my car.

"Take care." I waved.

Chapter Twenty-Six

Currently 2035…

Before I knew it, it had been ten more years. It was summer all year round in Phoenix, so the years flew by like nothing. No one came looking for me anymore. I spent many years unharmed. Occasionally, a vampire would come to town and end up dead by my blade. Not often anymore, but it happened. I wanted to make sure that I was the only vampire in the city and for the most part, I succeeded. I always left a few alive on one condition. They were to report to me if anyone had a male child by the name Erick. Very few got back to me once they left. I had a reputation now and they knew who I was the moment I showed up unannounced. I had Draven to thank for that. His journals of the battles in Romania and my powers were shared within the supernatural community. I don't know how much of it our people really believed since it was over twenty three years ago.

Stakes were no longer viable. They didn't do the trick with the new generation of vampires. They were stronger than any I had faced in my many years as a vampire. As crazy, as it sounded, it was true. There were many hybrid vampires, creations of the old council I destroyed no doubt. I could not use my full potential without alerting the authorities. I didn't always succeed at killing that breed but none ever came back. I sought out a weapon specialist, also a bitter vampire, and together we created a new weapon to kill super-naturals with one shot. The wood from the Beech tree and pure silver fastened at the tip. I learned a lot over the years especially as a hunter.

Then the times changed again, vampires no longer feared me. They feared no one. Humans wanted to be vampires. Movies, games, books and TV shows were becoming more and more popular. There were covens and clubs and cults acting as such. It was getting harder to distinguish between human and vampire these days. Most times, I had to rely on their blood before I killed them. However, in recent times, real vampires tend to blend in really well. The more human blood they drank, the less I was able to distinguish between the two. Eventually hunting ceased to exist. I couldn't risk killing a vampire for fear of them being a human. Enough blood had been shed by my hand. The Hierarchy never came after me, never punished me for not hunting anymore. I figured I just became another blip on their radar. I was just some insolent vampire they cared less and less about.

My search to find Erick became non-existent. Every birth I attended with a child named Erick turned out to be a false alarm. What I didn't know was whether the Angels cloaked him or not. I was certain if he came back as he always had, there would be something for me to find. Erick's scent stayed with me. He always found me.

Eventually, I accepted the fact that Erick was lost to me. It broke my heart to give up the search but they did say that he would never remember me.

This time I moved to the city that never sleeps, Las Vegas. Somewhere I could blend in without a problem. Las Vegas seemed the perfect place to live out the rest of my life. Time tends to move slowly there. I quickly adapted with my new environment. I met a fellow vampire who was a chemical engineer and had created a lotion for vampires to be able to go in the sun. I bought a few hundred bottles and stored them in my cellar, not that I needed it. I always think to the future, since it is all I can look forward to these days. The world was forever changing. I still heard from Victoria once a year. She kept me updated on the new council members and their decisions. She always sent photo's so I knew who they were.

The new basic rules were;

1. Do not tell humans we exist. (Which I had no problems doing. I remember all too well how it turned out.)

2. Try not to fall in love with a human. (The latter posed as a much more difficult rule for most of my kind. Yes my kind, might as well accept that it is what it is. I can't change it, it's not like there is a cure or anything…)

3. Lastly do not turn any human. (I certainly did not have a problem with that one.) However others found that hard once they had fallen in love but the council had to approve first. Something Ambrose had a hard time doing when it came to me. Speaking of Ambrose, the buzz

was he never died. Apparently, he got out after the Council went after us but when he arrived, everyone was dead.

Traitor … perhaps.

I don't know why I ever trusted him. Victoria told me she ran into him a few years back he had asked to join the council. Then I never heard much from her again.

Vegas deemed worthy of my stay. I kept busy. Found a small practice to join. I still had my degree in psychiatry but it had been over forty-five years since I received it. So, I had someone in Las Vegas, doctor me up a new birth certificate and drivers licence as well as alter my degree. I found a worthy partner and asked if I could join her practice until I got on my feet. A few years would never alert her to my condition. Just long enough to gather enough clients to start my own practice.

Her name was Dr. Julia Stone and she mainly dealt with people who had gambling problems; sounds cheesy but not at all surprising. I could not hide in my dungeon forever. I needed to get out before I became like Ambrose, bitter and repressed.

As for my new job and partner, Dr. Stone was a great psychiatrist and she became a great friend. I did keep my distance for a long time though. I did not socialize late hours or on weekends, but lunch or a quick dinner after work every now and again for novelty sake was okay in my book. I did not want to seem too much of a prude or it would raise questions that I did not want to answer. Then like always, things got complicated. One night after work, Julia decided to bombard me with questions. I think glamouring rather than running was easier.

"So tell me Sarah, why is it you choose to be single?" She asked her first question of the night.

We had known each other for two years and I had never once introduced her to a man in my life. Mainly because I did not have one, I did lie about one or two though.

"I'm not single, I'm dating someone. He goes away on business a lot." I sighed, hoping she bought my act.

"You are a fine actress Sarah." She teased. "So when do I get to meet this lucky man?" She smiled. Then it occurred to me, she was asking because she, herself was attracted to me. I did not need to read her thoughts to figure that out. I do not know why I never picked up on it before, maybe too preoccupied with hiding my truth that I failed to notice hers.

"Oh, I—I'm not sure, he may be in town this weekend." I replied.

"I see, well then bring him over to my soiree this Saturday. I throw one, twice a year with my friends and colleagues." She laughed.

"I will see what I can do." I paused trying to think up a good excuse.

I needed to find a man, fast.

"All work and no play makes Sarah a dull girl." She chided.

"How original Julia." I replied then glanced at my watch. "I should go. I have a friend stopping by," another lie, well not entirely. Okay, not so much as a friend more like a—well—a delivery boy with a box of frozen blood.

"Oh—you have friends other than me. Why don't you bring him or her with you?" She said. Her sarcasm was a little annoying.

There was no point in lying again, "I will let them know." I smiled and nodded. "See you tomorrow."

"Good night Sarah." She wiggled her fingers in a wave. I stared at her a long moment. Wishing I was capable of just going home with her for a night to keep her quiet. Honestly, it had been so long that I really would have considered it, if I had not taken the vow to never get involved intimately with a human again.

The drive home felt like the longest in a while. I went directly to my home and paced until my mind would ease. I contemplated erasing her memory and moving away, but that would mean I had to start over again. She was a harmless human that knew nothing. I still had a few years ahead of me before she began to question anything that would expose me.

Dusk had arrived and Julie called. She wanted to apologize for prying into my personal life. I explained that it was fine and we would be there this weekend. She seemed thrilled about it and let me go. Now my plan was to hit the clubs and pick me up a half decent man.

Club after club, night after night and the weekend was already here. I was out of options. The men at the bars were just too—idiotic and not my type at all. If I brought any of them to Julia's, she would see right through the façade. If I glamoured them it would see fake.

Chapter Twenty-Seven

It was about noon on Saturday and I had stopped at a local café for a black coffee to warm up. Anyone that touched me when I did not feed often would get the shock of their lives. My skin was like ice. Regardless of the weather, my skin only warmed when I fed on fresh blood. Alcohol helped some but it clouded my judgement and I needed that at its best. It was slim pickings here in Las Vegas. My diet consisted of coyotes, wild dogs and the occasional ram. Coyotes were such despicable creatures. If I wanted to go on a real hike, I went after the rams that hid in the rocky hills. But the only thing that would warm my blood was a fresh human donor. Animal blood only lasted for a few days if that. It was like take out but for vampires. While I sat, at this little café, incoherent thoughts began to seep into my mind and when I looked up, they became clearer. A man a few tables over, was having lunch with a—friend from what I could tell. I felt myself blush. He was thinking about me. I smiled at him once, our eyes locked and I knew he was the one. It would not take long for me to compel him to join me for the soiree and prime him up for the act.

He waved me over, which I reacted to with a pleasant half smile. I nodded in acceptance and walked over leaving money on the table with my empty cup of coffee. He watched my every move as I made my way over and stood next to him. I could tell he was very interested.

"Hi there," I said. He smiled again. Then he held out his hand to introduce me to his friend. When I glanced down, I gasped.

'NO!' I screamed in my head. *'It can't be.'* I backed away and practically ran into the fence.

"What's wrong?" He asked.

"I'm sorry I have to go I—" Don't believe it, is what I wanted to say.

'Hello Chère.' He chortled.

How did he find me?

He had been looking for me and I knew that now just by the look on his face. I reached my car just as he grabbed my arm.

"What's the hurry?" The man he was with asked.

"What do you want Ambrose?" I asked spinning around to face him.

"It has been a long time Sarah, are you still angry with me?" he grinned.

"Angry! I thought you were dead until Victoria told me otherwise a few years ago. It would appear that you betrayed us." I scoffed.

"No one betrayed anyone." He replied.

"Whatever, if you have nothing of importance to say then I need to get going." I turned away.

"Well I was hoping for a much more loving reunion but never the less. You are always trying to be the one in control." He leaned in real close, his breath kissed my ear.

"What?" I gasped practically choking on the word.

"You smell as sweet as I remember Chère." His lips touched my flesh and I felt my skin burn. My body reacted to the intimate touch of his kiss. I was instantly aroused and wanted him, bad. "You want me. Admit it." He whispered in my ear. His arm wrapped around my waist and the other slinked up by back into my hair.

"Like a hole in the head." I tried to push away. He pulled me to him again and I felt his breath on my neck. Instant shivers went up my spine. The burning between my legs alerts me. "What is going on?" I tried to break free again.

"I told you."

"What happened to the bond?" I gasped while he kissed my neck.

"I don't know." He gasped. "That I am not sure. After the battle, when I came too, I couldn't feel you in me anymore." He replied.

"Ahh, " I gasped as the roughness of his hands stop on my breasts.

"Au revoir Chère." He chortled.

"What! Where are you going? You can't just leave after… that." I gasped.

"Sure I can." He said inching closer. He knew how powerful I was, yet I still feared him. No matter how many times he had been killed in the past he never stayed dead. No matter how many times I vowed to stay away from him I wanted him.

"Let's go back to my place." I replied. He smiled and told his little follower to go.

We drove to my house where our clothes were ripped from our bodies and we had animal sex on the hallway floor. It had been way to long for me. "Why did you come find me?" I asked.

"I had to see for myself, what you had become. You are my fledgling." He sat up.

"I felt the connection between us end. I thought you were dead. " I said feeling overly exposed right now. Ambrose had a way of doing that.

"Oh they tried to kill me, that is true but they did not succeed. What everyone fails to remember is that my maker was a very powerful man and it took a lot to kill him. I am not so easily killed." He laughed.

"I will try to remember that." I stood and grabbed my clothes off the floor. He came up behind me his arms wrapped around my waist.

"I love you." he whispered then let go.

"So you say." I scoff. I dress then turn to face him. He is fully clothed. "You cut off all your hair." I walked closer. "Looks good," I smile. He smiles like a little kid then heads to the door.

"I'll see you around." he says. I stand in the door way and he turns one last time. "By the way Chase did not die."

My eyes widened and I feel like my world is spinning out of control, "How do you know he is not dead?" I asked. He laughed as he ran his fingers along the hood of my car.

He cocked his head, "With all that money this is the lemon you buy?" He shook his head.

"I don't need pretty things to please me Ambrose." I scowl. He is back to his old self. Why do I bother with him? I scold myself.

"Oh that's right, you are used to trash." He shrugged

"Ugh, are you here just to annoy me?" I growled.

"I told you—"

"You've told me a lot of things Ambrose. It doesn't mean I believe anything you say." My heart is racing.

"I see." He smirked.

I turn around and walk away, but before I go back in the house I asked, "Why after thirty years you decide to show yourself to me?"

"You were hard to track down. You never stayed in one place long enough for my trackers to find you." He replied.

"Trackers… Really Ambrose," I replied.

"I had things to take care of. I couldn't follow you around the country." He laughed.

"Too bad, it was quite the journey and maybe I could have had the chance to finally kill you." I replied.

"If the council failed to kill me, I doubt very much you could." He sneered confidently.

"I have invested my time in new weapons, Ambrose I am still a hunter."

"I heard," he chuckled.

"You've changed the subject once again. I asked you a question." I stood half in the door.

"Why does it matter?" He stated.

"I want to know the truth. Is Chase alive?" I replied.

"I have already answered that question!" He said.

"Don't come back here again." I replied.

"Who's gonna stop me?" He lunged for me again but this time I was ready. I was able to my gun. I aimed it at his chest.

"Do you really think that a few bullets will hurt me? Come on Sarah, I know that you are not that dumb." He laughed.

"Who said they were regular bullets?" I said and shot him. The look on his face was priceless. He was shocked that I even shot him and that I was right. The bullet was no regular bullet.

I knelt down in front of him, "I want nothing to do with you. If you know what is good for you, do not find me again." I stood and walked away.

*****

Sacramento California was the next place on my list. I cried the entire way there. I could hide out for a while. Over populated with people young and old, I could blend in no problem. If Ambrose followed me here, it would be too much of a bother for him search every corner of the city. Then again, did Ambrose ever give up? I stopped at a busy hotel and gave them a fake name and credit card. I also asked for the local paper. I cloaked the room, so he couldn't find me, *if* he tried. It worked on the council and their fiends so it should work on him. I tried to call Victoria again. There was no answer. I was praying that she was still in good health. I circled all the potential apartments in the local paper.

I called to say good bye to Julia and leave the life I had created, behind. She was sad to see me go but understood that when opportunity knocks you don't ignore it. Or so I told her. Then went to bed

*****

Sleep was almost impossible the next following weeks. I did however find a loft above an old warehouse.

I settled in and did all that I could to cloak the place. It had been two weeks and no sign of Ambrose. Every week I redid the cloaking spell. I even disguised myself, if I was leaving the house for more than a few hours. I could not underestimate his abilities. Then a month had gone by and still no sign of Ambrose. Any vampire for that matter and I was not sure if that was a good thing or a bad thing. I ended up going through three rentals before I felt safe. After the fourth location and fifth month, I convinced myself he was gone. He wanted to scare me and he did.

I spent the latter months of the year training with a martial arts expert, to gain better dexterity. I could never be too prepared. If Ambrose could show up out-of-the-blue, after all these years, who knows what would happen next. I also practiced with a weapons expert using guns and crossbows, which I liked better than stakes. I also found a live donor that I could glamour once a week. The blood clinic was an easy fix. I volunteered there once a week and took bags at the end of the night.

My apartment was well suited for an army barracks. I had reinforced metals doors, installed and an alarm system that required a retinal scan. Money well spent. The only thing I did not manage to create was a personal life. We all have a means to an end.

L.A became my final home. I had no intentions on leaving any time soon for any reason. I was alone and powerful, the new problem that arose lately was the blood lust. I began to enjoy the hunt more than I expected. It was something I knew would creep up on me eventually, when I least expected it.

Epilogue:

I had been enjoying the fast life of L.A, where people never age, thanks to cosmetic surgery. No one would ever question how young I still looked. Men were easily attracted to me which, made blood so easy to come by. Glamouring my subjects became easier with time. Money was becoming scarce. I had to find other ways of getting money, without working a regular job in a non-supernatural city. It wasn't always the most legal ways of getting money, but it worked. Men were the easiest prey. I was thankful that I knew they wouldn't come find me the next day when their bank accounts were emptied. At least my targets were high profile billionaires. I'm sure the wives didn't appreciate the millions that went missing. I had to start somewhere. Besides I only did it twice in the past forty years. The news was calling me the millionaire bandit for a while. Then I kept a low profile and really watched my spending habit.

Today I was walking down Rodeo drive, something I did often on my way home from the blood bank, and I spotted the most beautiful necklace in a store window. I pondered it for a while whether I should run in and buy it. It had been years since the millionaire bandit was mentioned so no one would suspect anything I purchased. I talked myself into buying it. As I walked out of the store, I spotted someone walk by, that I swear I recognized. I did a double take, there was little time for them to just disappear but whoever I just saw was gone. I scanned the streets with my vampire eyes and found nothing.

"Chase?" I whispered to myself in disbelief. I jogged down the street in the direction of the person I saw, catching only a glimpse of him at every corner. He never glanced my way but he quickened his pace. The next set of lights he turned down a street. I crossed the street to follow him. He did not turn around but he realized suddenly that I was there and stopped walking. I didn't understand what was going on. I tried to catch my breath and calm my palpitating heart while still watching for him. I stepped forward just as steam rushed out of the vents. That was when I felt someone come up behind me, my one arm in its grasp and then I felt steel on my throat.

"Why are you following me?" He asked.

English accent gone, he looked exactly as I remembered him.

"Erick?" I replied. My eyes filled my tears. "What the—?"

"Why are you following me?" He repeated, pushing me up against the brick wall, the silver blade cutting my throat.

"I wasn't following you Erick, I-I was following someone else?" He pushed me away but kept the dagger pointing at me. I scanned the area with my eyes.

"Why are you calling me Erick?" He asked.

"Huh? Well isn't that your name?"

"Uh—no it isn't lady! Who sent you?" He demanded.

'Sneaky little angels,' I groaned under my breath. He attempted to charge at me but I lunged for him giving myself the upper hand. I pushed him against the wall then backed away a far distance from his blade.

"What are you talking about? Why would anyone send me after you?" I asked, but remained calm. "What is your name if it isn't Erick?"

"My name is none of your business and if you are what I think you are then you must die." He was not afraid of me at all. He lunged for me but someone came out of nowhere and stopped him.

"Stop!" He shouted. My eyes widened as my head slowly turned to look at the familiar voice that just spoke. It was as if my life was flashing before my eyes.

"Chase?" I could not believe it.

"Hello Sarah." He smiled. My eyes blinked a few times. This could not be happening? Where has he been? "Sarah?" My heart stopped. I started to feel faint. "I see you haven't changed." Chase chortled.

*****

When I came too, Chase was sitting across from me on the coffee table. I sat up and said, "Déjà vu." He laughed and reached out to touch me. I jumped back, frightened.

"Are you really here or am I having vision." The tears welled in my eyes. "Well I guess if I am having a vision you wouldn't answer my question properly anyway so—"

"Calm down." He laughed. "I am really here." He replied with his sexy little smile. Oh my god I missed that smile. I bit down on my bottom lip.

"How did you know where I lived?" I asked. He grinned. I swooned. How I missed his face.

"You here to stay," I asked hope full.

"Yes. There is no one that will stop me this time." He took my hands in his. He leaned in and I could feel the heat emanating from him then Erick came into view, rubbing his head looking confused.

"What's the deal with him?" I asked thumbing over my shoulder.

"His name is Samuel and yes, it is Erick." He replied craning his neck to look over at him.

"Wow . . . it's amazing how he looks just like he did forty years ago." I replied.

"Amazing huh," His one brow rose.

"You know what I mean." I rolled my eyes at him.

"He remembers nothing." Chase sighed. "I really don't know if that is a good thing yet."

"Why are you with him?"

"I found him one day wandering around the streets at night and I have been sort of following him ever since. Then he moved out on his own and was given this role, again." Chase explained.

"Does he know what you are?"

"Probably . . . He has no idea that I was once his brother though."

"Are you going to tell him that part?" I asked.

"No, now that I have found you all I care about is making up for lost time. Nothing else matters." He kissed me and my heart started to race like crazy.

"So am I good to go?" Samuel asked standing in the hallway knuckles on his hips.

"Yes." Chase replied. I stood up as did Chase. He pulled me to him. I was still in shock that he was standing in front of me. I giggled like a school girl and felt the blood rush to my cheeks.

"Thank you for not staking me." I glanced back in Erick's direction.

"Chase said you are one of the good ones. I trust him." He replied. "Guess you found what you were looking for huh." Erick smiled hauling his duffle bag over his shoulder.

"Take care of yourself, Samuel." I took his hand in mine and gave it a gentle shake. His eyes blinked and he stepped away from my touch. His lips parted and he inhaled. He looked as though he had just seen a ghost. I turned to look at Chase but he had not noticed. He stood there and stared at me. I walked towards the door and as it opened I spotted Ambrose. I tossed Erick away just as Ambrose grabbed me.

"Sarah." He hissed.

"Why do you keep pestering me?" Was all I could spit out. Erick jumped to his feet with stake in his hand.

"One big happy family back together again huh." He growled.

"What now Ambrose?"

"You tried to kill me and you ask me, what now?" He scoffed. "Did you really think it would be that easy to get rid of me?" Erick watched us banter, from the other side of the couch, prepared for anything.

"Let her go Ambrose." Chase demanded.

"Don't you boys ever tire of this game?" He shouted.

"What is he talking about?" Erick replied. I glanced over at him watching him look down at his hands then back up at me.

"I mean, come—on. The same girl century after century, doesn't it lose its luster?" He laughed.

"Get out!" I replied.

"What? I can't visit an old friend." He remarked.

"Friend? Have you gone completely mad Ambrose? You have no friends here." I replied inching forward. I should have put a bullet in your head!"

"Oh that's right, you tried to kill me."

"You've tried to kill him?" Erick blurted. "I thought you all stuck together?"

"What's wrong with him? Isn't he British?" Ambrose asked looking at Erick confused. Chase laughed.

I ignored Ambrose's comments, "I've killed him many times, unfortunately this one, no matter the attempts, never fucking dies." I pulled free of his grasp and leapt over the couch again, keeping a safe distance between us. "How long did you know I was here?"

"I have been following you for a few decades Chère." Ambrose replied. "You can never escape me, I told you that."

"This is going to end here and now." I shouted grabbing the shotgun from the closet.

"Good to see you finally found each other." Ambrose winked at me.

"You knew?" Chase looked at me queerly.

"I didn't believe him! I figured if you were alive you would have found me already." I shrugged.

"I tried to reach out to you so many times and I thought I had reached you then you just got farther away and harder to find." He sighed.

"You were the whispers?" I gasped. He smiled at me relieve. My heart was breaking all over again. I heard every whisper, but I believed that I was either losing my mind or Ambrose had been taunting with me.

"See." Ambrose Chided.

"If I believed it, maybe I would have searched for you. I'm sorry Chase. " I cried.

"Understandable, Ambrose is not the most trustworthy of—friend or foe?" Chase nodded in agreement.

"Foe—always foe," I corrected. "I just want to be left alone. Why can't you just leave me alone?" I screamed.

"Love works in mysterious ways don't you think." Ambrose attempted to come at me again but I let off a round in his chest. I watched as he slowly dropped to his knees, blood seeping from the wound.

"You have no idea about love." I spat at him. "By the way the wood will splinter and make its way to your heart. That's what's so great about a shotgun with exploding wooden bullets. Shrapnel is hard to pick out." I smiled.

"Huh?" Ambrose groaned clenching his chest.

"Lucky for you I don't have time to watch you suffer." I opened the broom closet and unsheathed my silver sword.

"Sarah?" Tears welled in his eyes. "I-I love you."

"No—you love the idea of loving me Ambrose, you could never actually love anyone." I replied and severed his head. "Take his body and burn it. Then scatter his ashes in different places." I said to Chase and Samuel replacing the sword in its sheath after cleaning it. They both nodded. I could see in Chase's expression that I intimidated him now. I was a different. Not the woman he fell in love with so long ago.

When Chase returned he was alone. He said his farewell to Samuel and returned to me unscathed. His hands cupped my face the instant we were alone. I did all I could not to break down in front of him.

"You've changed." He hugged me.

"I had to." I replied.

"I am sorry this has happened to you." He kissed my cheek. I didn't reply. We had been through this so many times before and I knew he never wanted this life for me. I know he hated that Ambrose destroyed me.

"I—I can't believe you're here." I cried.

"I'm here and this time it's to stay." He said.

I hugged him for a long time. His lips touched mine and that was it for me. I had to have him before he slipped through my fingers again. One thing I have learned since meeting vampires, they say one thing and do the complete opposite.

Later that night I went to hunt alone. On my way back I ran into Samuel. He greeted me happily.

"Where's Chase?" He asked looking over his shoulder.

"Back at the condo," I smiled. "I thought you would have left town by now?" I added.

"I couldn't." He said rather shortly.

"Is everything alright?" I asked walking with him down the street.

"No, everything is not alright—Sarah." He stopped and stood in front of me, and for the first time in a long time, I saw the man that I had thought I had lost forever.

I blinked. "Erick?" I gasped. He didn't say anything, he didn't move, he just gave me a half smile. "How," I asked.

"When you touched me, just before Ambrose arrived," He replied.

"I thought I saw something change in you. Why didn't you say something before?" I was more excited than I should have been.

"I didn't want Chase to know that I remembered." He looked away. "I know you have been waiting a long time to rekindle what you have lost. I didn't want to interfere."

"Then why tell me now, here, where we are alone?" I suddenly felt, nervous. Afraid of what Erick might do.

"Chase wouldn't understand." He moved closer.

"Understand what?" I stuttered backing away.

"That you can never, really be together." He stopped walking and I turned to face him.

I started to panic, "What do you mean?" Just then Erick staked me. I looked down at my chest in shock. "Erick?" I cried. Images flashed through my head.

"I'm sorry Sarah. This is for the greater good. One day you'll understand." He leaned down as I fell and kissed my forehead. "I love you." He cried. "They will take you and cleanse your soul for rebirth." He knelt in front of me. "I should have done this long ago." I stared at him shocked. "I should never have let my love for you interfere with our true mission." Everything around me began to blur and fade away but the images in my mind flickered rapidly. Images that didn't even make sense to me but I was part of all of them.

"I loved you." Tears fell effortlessly from my eyes. Then I felt a sense of peace and let myself go.

"It will be all over soon my love." He whispered in my ear.

"I don't understand," I whispered.

"You will my love, you will." He let me go and it felt as though I was floating. It was the same feeling I felt when I died giving birth to Alaina.

Eremial

"Her body, where did you leave it," someone with a deep voice asked.

"I buried her in a cemetery."

"Very well. Let us get started." Azazel replied. "Eremial, please prepare Lailah for the ceremony." He commanded then left the room. Sarah looked at Eremial confused. He took her hand and exited the room.

"Your mission was unsuccessful. You are one of the chosen angels, Lailah. If you cannot get it right this time. Your reign will end."

"What—am I supposed to do?" Sarah asked.

"This I cannot tell you. You have to search within yourself to find the answers. You did everything right before, only you became a vampire, as did your *heir*." He stressed the word heir and it was then Sarah realized what she had to do. "This cannot happen again."

Sarah was to bare the child who would be the most powerful being on earth, the rebirth of our savoir. The being would destroy all that was unholy. Alaina should have been this being, only she was created from evil, not good. Sarah eyes watered as she remembered her daughters face.

"I will find you again. I promise." He kissed her then left.   It was thoroughly explained to Sarah that her mission could not fail again or the evil in the world would reign. There could not be another failure with her mission. Erick was determined to make sure that Chase would not find her again. He had put her life in danger many times before. Lailah *'Sarah'* dressed in a white gown then followed the Seraphim to the great hall to meet with the Hierarchy. When she entered all Arch Angels turned to greet her.

"Lailah, we are sending you back one more time. Please do not fail us." Azazel replied. He walked towards Sarah and hugged her lovingly. "Dear sister, I do not want to cease your existence."

"I understand." Sarah replied like a drone and with his last kiss; she was reborn ….

Lailah

The last thing I remembered was a heartbeat, darkness and warm wet liquid surrounding me. Then suddenly there was a bright white light blinding me. I was being pulled by something large and cold. There was a brief sharp pain in my chest as I tried to breath and then—I began to cry.

I was placed on my mother's chest and she called me, Zara.

THE END

Authors Notes:

Thank you all for taking the time to read my series. I really hope you enjoyed it. It was a pleasure sharing this story with all of you. I would have loved to continue this series, and perhaps in the near future, I may create one last hurrah for Sarah. For now I need to venture towards a new genre until I find the right agent.

Sincerely,

S.L Ross

You can always stop by my blog at
http://sabrinaross.blogspot.com/ for updates on what's to come.

Follow me on twitter **@SL_Ross**

Facebook fanpage @ **http://tinyurl.com/immortalislandseries**

I am always willing to hear your thoughts or thoughts on my book.

sl_ross@rogers.com

S.L Ross has a passion for writing and creating an alternate universe in her work. She has been writing since she was a child and always dreamed of becoming a published Author. Immortal Island is her first released novel series in the fiction genre.

Made in the USA
Charleston, SC
06 August 2012